The Golden Feather

Amanda McCabe

Ⓢ
A SIGNET BOOK

SIGNET
Published by New American Library, a division of
Penguin Putnam Inc., 375 Hudson Street,
New York, New York 10014, U.S.A.
Penguin Books Ltd, 80 Strand,
London WC2R 0RL, England
Penguin Books Australia Ltd, Ringwood,
Victoria, Australia
Penguin Books Canada Ltd, 10 Alcorn Avenue,
Toronto, Ontario, Canada M4V 3B2
Penguin Books (N.Z.) Ltd, 182–190 Wairau Road,
Auckland 10, New Zealand

Penguin Books Ltd, Registered Offices:
Harmondsworth, Middlesex, England

Published by Signet, an imprint of New American Library,
a division of Penguin Putnam Inc.

First Printing, November 2002
10 9 8 7 6 5 4 3 2 1

Copyright © Ammanda McCabe, 2002

Printed in the United States of America

PUBLISHER'S NOTE
This is a work of fiction. Names, characters, places, and incidents either
are the product of the author's imagination or are used fictitiously,
and any resemblance to actual persons, living or dead, business
establishments, events, or locales is entirely coincidental.

BOOKS ARE AVAILABLE AT QUANTITY DISCOUNTS WHEN USED TO PROMOTE
PRODUCTS OR SERVICES. FOR INFORMATION PLEASE WRITE TO PREMIUM
MARKETING DIVISION, PENGUIN PUTNAM INC., 375 HUDSON STREET, NEW
YORK, NEW YORK 10014.

A Lady of Mystery

She wore a black silk mask that covered all her face except for her full red lips and an alabaster jawline. Her hair, a deep burgundy-red color, was piled atop her head in curls and whorls. The emeralds in her ears winked and dazzled in the light.

Mrs. Archer was very striking. And she did indeed have a magnificent bosom, its whiteness set off by the low bodice of her green satin gown.

Justin very much feared he was gaping, just as everyone else in the room was. But he couldn't help himself; she was such a terribly striking sight.

Then Mrs. Archer came down the stairs, her skirt held up daintily to reveal green heeled slippers and the tiniest amount of white silk stocking, and moved into the crowd.

Justin could see only the very top of her head as she walked about, stopping to speak to various patrons and accept a glass of champagne from a footman.

He blinked and turned quickly away, feeling as if he were trapped in some bizarre, terribly attractive dream.

In memory of my grandmother Roberta McCabe, who always said she just knew I'd be a writer someday.

I wish you were here to see this now, Nana.

Prologue

London, 1810

"Am I dead, then?" Justin Seward leaned back against the cushions of the jolting carriage and reached an unsteady hand up to touch the aching hole in his shoulder. His fingers came away a sticky red.

"Don't be ridiculous, man!" his friend the Honorable Freddie Reed said heartily. "It's barely a scratch. Old Holmes could never shoot worth a farthing. We'll have you home in a trice."

James Burne-Jones, who sat across from them, snickered. "You may not be dead, Justin," he said, "but you'll surely wish you were once your father hears of this. Remember how he shouted the last time!"

Justin groaned again and closed his eyes tightly. Oh, yes. His father, the grand Earl of Lyndon, was sure to ring a mighty peal over him for this, Justin's third duel in a year. After the second one, the earl had threatened any number of dire consequences if he ever heard of his son causing any more such scandals. The very walls had shaken with his wrath.

Justin almost asked his friends to turn back around so that he could ask Holmes to finish what he started. Death was preferable to whatever awaited him at Seward House.

He tried to stay out of trouble, truly he did. For months he had avoided all his usual haunts: the gaming hells, the clubs, the racetrack. How was he to know that Pamela Holmes, who had been sending him provocative, violet-scented letters, had a jealous husband who would be waiting when Justin showed up for their rendezvous—and who would call him out?

Truly, trouble just seemed to seek him out, and had ever since he left Cambridge two years ago.

Unlike his perfect older brother, Edward, Viscount Keir, who never took a step wrong.

The carriage lurched to a halt outside Seward House. It looked quiet, as though all were asleep in the pale early-morning light, but Justin knew better. He knew that divine retribution awaited him in those dignified walls. He had slid neatly out of trouble a dozen times before. This time was different. This time he had used up his last, and probably best, chance.

A deep shame washed over him, burying even the pain in his shoulder and the hot rush of temper he had felt at Holmes's challenge. Shame was a rare emotion for Justin; it was so easy to shrug off his parents' anger, to hurry on to the next adventure. Now he was drowning in it, in the weight of his parents' destroyed expectations, of his own disappointment in himself.

He had gone too far this time, and he knew it. He also knew that not even another horse race, another fight, another woman could ever take away the bitter taste of the ashes of dreams. His parents had expected so much of him, and he had let them down over and over again.

"Here we are now, old man!" said Freddie. "Home again."

Richards, the butler, emerged from the house and hurried down the steps to open the carriage door. "Mr. Seward!" he cried, his eyes widening at the sight of blood. "Oh, Mr. Seward, are you badly injured, then? I shall send for the doctor at once!"

Freddie and James seized Justin between them and lowered him to the ground. His legs buckled, and he would have fallen to the pavement if they had not hauled him upright.

"No need for a doctor, Richards," he managed to gasp. "It is nothing at all. . . ."

His voice trailed away as he looked up the steps to the open door. His mother stood there, leaning heavily against the door frame.

Amelia, the Countess of Lyndon, had not been well for some time. Her face was pale and faded above the neck frill of her dark blue dress, and she looked as if a strong wind could carry her away at any moment. She pressed a handkerchief to her mouth.

Standing behind her, his eyes shining with excitement, was Justin's younger brother Harry. His older brother Edward was, as usual, off on some responsible, respectable task.

"Justin," his mother said softly, brokenly, "you are alive! I was so afraid for you."

The shame that had overtaken him in the carriage was now well nigh crippling. He was glad of his friends' strong arms supporting him. If they did not hold him up, he feared he would fall down at his mother's feet, weeping and begging forgiveness.

And Harry—Harry should not be here to see this. He was far too impressionable already.

Freddie and James helped him up the steps, trailed by the fluttering, fussing Richards. They went past Amelia and Harry and deposited Justin on one of the satin-upholstered chairs that lined the cavernous marble foyer. Then they beat a hasty retreat.

The cowards.

"Of course I am not dead, Mother," he said, as she bent over him to wipe at his shoulder with the handkerchief. "Holmes is a terrible shot. And you should be in bed, asleep."

"How can I stay abed, when I do not know if my son is alive or dead? I had to know."

"Was it a good fight, Justin?" Harry broke in excitedly. "How I wish I could have been there!"

Amelia turned a horrified gaze onto her youngest son.

"It was very dull and stupid, Harry," Justin muttered. "You were well away from it."

"No!" Harry protested. "Next time, I will be there with you, as your second. . . ."

"You will do no such thing, Harold," a voice boomed across the foyer. "Do you want to be as big a dolt as your brother? I will send you away to university in Scotland first!"

Everyone's gaze turned to the shadows at the foot of the grand staircase. A man, tall, erect, silver haired, emerged from them into the murky light from the small windows.

Harry's face turned scarlet. "Sir! I only meant—"

"I know what you meant," the earl said. "Don't be an ass. Take your mother back upstairs, and have her maid give her some of her medicine."

"I want to stay here, Walter," Amelia said quietly.

The earl's face gentled as he came up to his wife and took her hand. "You know the doctor said you should not leave your bed, Amelia. The strain of all this has been too great for you. Please, my dear, go with Harold, and let Minette give you your medicine."

Amelia glanced uncertainly at Justin. Then, under the quiet weight of her husband's command, she nodded and took Harry's arm, allowing him to escort her up the stairs. She only looked back once, lingeringly.

"Richards," the earl said, when they had disappeared from sight, "would you be so good as to fetch Dr. Reynolds? Tell him both Lady Lyndon and Mr. Seward are in need of his services."

"Yes, my lord, right away." Richards bowed, and scurried quickly away.

Justin was left alone with his father.

The earl sat down in the chair next to his and said very softly, "You have gone too far this time, you know, Justin."

Justin bowed his head. Somehow, the quiet resignation in his father's voice was far worse than any thunder or noise. "Yes, Father. I know."

"I paid your debts at that dreadful gaming hell. I paid off the opera dancer who was getting so pushing. I concealed your other duels. Everyone is young and foolish once in their lives. But I cannot go on. You have brought scandal and disgrace onto the Seward name, a name that has been held in highest respect for over three hundred years."

Sharp tears prickled at the backs of Justin's eyes.

He blinked them away furiously. No amount of tears could cleanse the stain of his life.

"I am through with all that, sir," he said roughly. "I promise."

The earl shook his head. "That is what you told us the last time. And the time before that. I fear a change must be made."

A chill of foreboding shivered on Justin's spine. "What sort of a change?"

The earl reached inside his coat and brought out a heavily sealed, deeply official-looking document. "I have purchased you a commission. As soon as you have recovered from your wound, you will go to India, where you will serve in the regiment of my old friend, Colonel Paget."

India. He was being sent off to India. This was almost worse than anything he had imagined on that short but endless carriage ride. India was hot and insect-ridden and very, very far away.

Justin nodded in resignation. It was a dismal prospect, yes, to be so far from home, but perhaps there, in such an alien land, he could bring back to his family a small portion of the honor he had lost them.

"And that, I fear, Mrs. Aldritch, is all that is left."

Caroline Aldritch carefully folded her black-gloved hands in her lap and stared dispassionately across the desk at the sallow-faced attorney.

She should feel *something*, she knew, at the sure knowledge that she was now destitute. Obviously, the attorney expected her to swoon, since he was clutching a bottle of smelling salts in his hand. Or perhaps the salts were for himself, since he was the one who had to deal with the complicated wreckage of her husband's estate.

She should have been weeping or in hysterics, or throwing a fiery tantrum at the fate that had led her to this. Instead, the numbness that held her since she had been told of Lawrence's death still gripped her.

All she could think was, *I knew it.*

Her life with Lawrence could have ended no other way.

"So," she said, "after all my husband's debts are settled, I will be left with twenty pounds. More or less."

"Or perhaps a bit more. If we are careful," answered the attorney.

Caroline nodded. Twenty pounds could keep her in their shabby lodgings a while longer, to be sure. But it would not pay for Phoebe to stay at the privileged Mrs. Medlock's School for Young Ladies.

At the thought of Phoebe, her sweet younger sister, emotion did stir in Caroline's heart. Phoebe was happy at her school; her letters were always full of her lessons and outings and friends. She was meeting people there, young ladies of good family, who could serve her well in her future life. The only good thing Lawrence had ever done for Caroline in their marriage was to pay for Phoebe's schooling after their parents died, though heaven only knew how he did it.

There had to be a way to keep her there, to pay for a fine come-out one day. There *had* to be. Caroline would not see Phoebe end up as *she* had.

She stood abruptly, the folds of her black bombazine dress rustling around her. "Thank you," she said. "You have been very helpful."

The attorney walked with her to the door. "If there is anything else I can do, Mrs. Aldritch, please do not hesitate to call on me."

"I won't. Good day."

Caroline stepped out onto the pavement, shading her eyes against the sudden glare of sunlight. It was not a particularly bright day, but after the gloom of the office it seemed almost tropical. She lowered the veil of her bonnet and looked about for a hansom cab.

Then she remembered the pitifully few coins left in her reticule and decided to walk.

She was very nearly to the rooming house where she and Lawrence had their lodgings when she heard a voice, a man's voice, call out, "Mrs. Aldritch! Mrs. Aldritch, over here!"

Caroline looked over her shoulder to see a tall, vaguely familiar man making his way through the crowds toward her. He was a friend of Lawrence's, she knew; one of the friends he had gone to gaming hells and racetracks with, one of the friends she disliked. However, being rude now was sure to avail her nothing, so she paused, a polite smile on her lips.

"Mrs. Aldritch, thank goodness I have found you! Your landlady said you were out," he said, coming to a halt next to her. Caroline saw then that he held a small, paper-wrapped parcel under his arm.

"I had some business to attend to, Mr. . . ."

"Burne-Jones. Mr. James Burne-Jones. We met at the Bedford rout last month."

Caroline remembered that rout, given by some of the last members of very minor gentry who still welcomed Lawrence to their home. She remembered standing by the wall, watching the dancers while Lawrence lost desperately in the card room. She did not remember this man, but she said, "Yes, of course."

"Well, I am leaving Town this afternoon, but I could not go without giving you this." He thrust the parcel at her.

Caroline reached out for it slowly. "What? . . ."

"Oh, it is nothing improper at all, Mrs. Aldritch! It belonged to Larry. He left it with me for safekeeping, shortly before . . . before he died."

Died getting run down by a carriage, too foxed to look before he stepped into the street, Caroline thought wryly. The parcel was probably his watch, missing since he died, and maybe a few coins. "Thank you very much, Mr. Burne-Jones. It was kind of you to bring it to me."

"Anything for Larry's widow! We were all so sorry when he died. He was a good 'un, was Larry."

"Indeed," Caroline answered. Then she felt the tiny hairs on the back of her neck prickle. She looked back to see her landlady, Mrs. Brown, watching her suspiciously from between the curtains of her front window.

Caroline sighed. The very last thing she needed was to be tossed out of her already tenuous lodgings on suspicion of being a too-merry widow.

She quickly took her leave of Mr. Burne-Jones and hurried inside the tall, narrow house, clutching the parcel. She sped past the closed door of Mrs. Brown's sitting room and up the stairs, praying that she could avoid another confrontation about late rent payments for just a little longer. Just long enough so that she could think in peace.

Once inside the small suite of two rooms, Caroline shut and locked the door behind her and leaned back wearily against the flimsy wood. It was not even noon yet, but, lud, it felt like this horrible day would go on forever!

She took off her black bonnet and tossed it and her gloves onto the table. Then she sat down on the unmade bed and removed the paper wrappings from the parcel.

It was a box, a small tin box with a little key in the lock. Caroline ran her hand over the cool metal lid and shook the box slightly, listening to the metallic echo.

"Please, let there be enough here to pay the rent," she whispered. Then she turned the key, lifted the lid—and gasped.

Inside there were indeed some coins, along with a few banknotes. Quite enough to keep Mrs. Brown happy for a while longer. There was also a neatly folded piece of paper. Caroline pushed aside the money and took it out to read.

It was a deed. To a gaming establishment called the Golden Feather. It was signed over to Lawrence by the owner, a Mr. Samuels, won the very night Lawrence died. Tucked inside the paper was a heavy key.

How ironic. Poor Lawrence. He had possessed one of his few winning hands that night, but had not lived long enough to enjoy it.

Caroline lifted her gaze from the deed and looked over at where Lawrence's miniature portrait was propped on the narrow fireplace mantel.

The picture had been painted some years before, and the image that looked back at her was not that of her weary, red-eyed husband. It was her young bridegroom, with his clear green eyes full of idealism and honesty.

What hopes they'd had on their wedding day! How impatient they had been, how impulsive and in love. But they had been too young, only seventeen. And their love had not been able to survive their families' obligations and the poverty that had overtaken them. Both the Aldritches and the Lanes had been good families of faded fortunes; they had hoped their children would marry well—not elope with someone equally faded.

Caroline and Lawrence *had* loved each other once, or they thought they did. But not enough to sustain them through all their new and unexpected difficulties. Caroline had tried to make a home for them, but Lawrence had lost himself in the lures of gaming and drink. He had been convinced that if only his luck would turn, just once, if only he could win the next hand, he would be able to take care of them.

Caroline looked down at the deed in her hand. Maybe now, in a strange way, he *was* taking care of her, at long last.

But only if she had the courage to go out there and take care of herself.

Caroline looked at the paper she was holding and then back up at the building. Yes, this was it. The Golden Feather. Lawrence's legacy.

She would never have known it was a gaming establishment from the exterior. It looked like any other nondescript, respectable town house in a row of town houses. Someone had been looking after it; the front steps were swept, the brass door knocker polished, and the heavy curtains were drawn across the windows. The only indication of its true purpose was a small plate affixed beneath the knocker that read THE GOLDEN FEATHER—MEMBERS ONLY.

Caroline took a deep breath, turned the key in the lock, and went inside.

She had to pass through a small foyer, bare but for a desk and chair, to get to the main salon. She pulled back the window draperies of green velvet and looked about in surprised satisfaction. It was very grand indeed, with velvet and gilt chairs clustered about the card tables and the roulette wheel. Fine paintings hung on the silk-papered walls, and a thick green-and-gold carpet covered the floor.

Through an arched doorway she saw a dining room, equally grand. In the corner, a spiral staircase ran up to another floor. Perhaps there were rooms there that could be made into a private apartment.

How prosperous this Golden Feather must be, Caroline reflected, as she gave the roulette wheel an idle spin. She could just envision the crowds of well-dressed gamesters who would flock here, filling the gilt chairs, drinking champagne—spending their money.

She had thought perhaps to sell the place, to pay for Phoebe's remaining years at school from the proceeds. But if she could run it herself, just for a few years, how much more money they could have! Enough for a come-out and a fine dowry for Phoebe. Perhaps even a cozy country cottage for herself.

It would be simple enough to say that Lawrence had lost the deed soon to some mystery lady after winning it. She had come to enough places like this with her husband to know the basics of how they were run. She would need help, of course, but she was a fast learner. It could be done. And then she would never have to marry again, never be at the mercy of a careless, irresponsible man again.

But, oh, then she would have to live every day in a world she hated! A world she had blamed for ruining her husband, her marriage. Ruining the naive, romantic girl she had once been.

Caroline sat down in one of the velvet chairs and propped her chin on her black-gloved hand. She did hate gaming, but what choice did she really have? If she did not make use of this place, she would be utterly ruined. She had no job skills and certainly no matrimonial prospects. She would starve in the streets. Worse yet, Phoebe, her dear Phoebe, would be ruined along with her.

"It will not be forever," she whispered fiercely, convincing herself. "It will not be forever!"

Chapter One

London, Four Years Later

"Justin, you're home! You're home at last."

Justin, now the Earl of Lyndon on the deaths over a year ago of his father and older brother, barely had time to hand the butler his greatcoat when his mother came down the stairs. She enveloped him in her rose-scented embrace, holding him tightly.

"It has been so long," she murmured, her voice muffled against his shirtfront.

Justin rested his cheek against her ruffled lace cap. "Yes, Mother. Too long."

He had thought so many times during the hot, endless days in India that he would surely never be in this place again. Never see his family, never be in his home, never feel the coolness of a sweet English breeze on his face. England had seemed an impossible dream, so distant from the sticky, dusty Indian reality.

Yet here he was. Standing once again in the foyer of Seward House. It all looked the same. The same family portraits hung on the walls; the same faded Aubusson rug lined the floor. Richards was the same, trying to hide his undignified emotion behind a stolid facade. His mother even smelled the same, of roses and sugar cakes.

But she did not look the same, Justin thought as he drew back a bit to look at her. Amelia had been pale and sickly when he left four years ago. Almost like a shadow. Now she had gained some weight; her lavender silk gown lay smooth on her rounded shoulders. Her cheeks were a pale pink, her eyes sparkling with delight at her son's homecoming. She must have ceased taking the "medicine" she used to have.

"I started for home as soon as I received your letter about Father and Edward's accident, Mother," he said. "I'm sorry it has taken me so very long."

"I know, dear. It was so . . . so very difficult, all alone without them," Amelia said, with a rather watery smile. "You are here, though, and that is all that matters. I am certain all will be well now."

All would be well? "Mother, what? . . ."

Amelia shook her head. "Not now. I will tell you everything later, but right now you must be so tired. Come into the drawing room and have some tea. I want to hear all about your journey, and about India! How very brown you have become there, dear."

They were quickly settled in the elegant blue-and-silver drawing room, with a vast tray of tea, cakes, and sandwiches. Justin sat back and watched his mother pour out the tea, listening as she prattled happily about the Season just concluding and her plans for the summer ahead. When at last the final seedcake was eaten and Amelia had paused for breath, Justin said, "I suppose Harry is still at Cambridge, then."

Amelia's bright smile faded, and her gaze fell away from his.

A small chill touched Justin's weary heart. He leaned toward her, reaching out to catch her hand and cease her sudden fussing with the tea things. "Mother? Is something wrong with Harry? Is he ill?"

She shook her head. "No, he is not ill. It is just— oh, Justin! I *am* glad you are home. I simply don't know what to do."

Justin released her hand and sank back in his chair, folding his arms across his chest. "Mother, you must tell me, whatever it is."

"Harry has been sent down from Cambridge."

"Sent down! Well, surely there are appeals that can be made, people to speak to. . . ."

"It is the third time. They will not have him back."

Justin was appalled. Harry had been sent down from Cambridge *three* times? Even he himself, at the height of his mischief-making youth, had managed to stay at university.

Harry must have done something very bad indeed.

"When did this happen?" he asked quietly.

"Not long before your father died. He was livid with Harry, absolutely livid!" Amelia shuddered. "I had never seen Walter so angry."

Justin could well imagine. His father had dealt with one wayward son, only to have another spring up in his place.

He could only shake his head at the desperate foolishness of youth. Wisdom was so hard-won, especially in India. He hoped his brother could be spared a hard lesson like that. Perhaps his hopes were in vain; he knew how heedless a rakish youth could be.

And now his mother was looking to him to solve all their difficulties.

"What is Harry doing now?" he asked.

Amelia shrugged. "Not very much of anything, I believe. I seldom see him. He is not interested in going to Almack's with me, or to *respectable* balls and routs. I think . . . I think he has become quite a *rake*." Her cheeks flamed as she whispered the word. "I do hear such stories about him, though I am sure they cannot be true."

Justin groaned to himself. He had hoped that once he got home, once he left the strangeness of India behind, his life would be peaceful. That he could marry, raise a passle of brats, and be quiet and respectable at long last.

That was obviously not to be.

"The Season is over now, though," Amelia continued. "Surely things will be better once we are back in the country, at Waring Castle. There will be no bad influences for him there."

Justin rubbed wearily at his jaw. "He has agreed to go to Waring for the summer, then?"

"Not exactly. But I am sure that now you are home, you can persuade him."

Justin was not so sure. He remembered all too well the determination of a headstrong boy set on being a rake. He also knew the terrible consequences of such heedlessness.

"I will see what I can do, Mother," he said.

She nodded, seemingly satisfied. "There is one more ball before absolutely everyone leaves Town, and I think we should attend. My friend Lady Bellweather has the loveliest daughter who just made her bow this Season. I am sure you would like her. . . ."

Her words faded away as the drawing-room door flew open and Harry rushed in. His hair, a darker brown than Justin's own sun-touched locks, fell in an untidy tangle over his brow, and he was in need of a shave. But it was really his clothes that made Justin's brow raise. Harry wore canary-yellow breeches below a purple—purple!—waistcoat, and a bottle-green coat.

And were those *parrots* embroidered on that waistcoat?

Justin knew then that they had more trouble than his mother thought.

"So you're home at last, eh, Justin?" Harry said, sauntering over to drape himself across the chair next to his mother's. He stuffed the last of the cucumber sandwiches into his mouth and chewed, grinning the whole time. "I see you were too wily for those old natives! Didn't even get stepped on by an elephant."

"Indeed," Justin answered slowly. "It is good to see you again, Harry."

Harry laughed. "I suppose Mother has been telling you all about those toads at Cambridge chucking me out."

"Something of the sort."

"Well, they had no business to do it, I can tell you! It was all a harmless hum. A misunderstanding."

"Your third misunderstanding, apparently."

"Yes, well, *you* know how it goes. These things happen. But it's given me time for more . . . edifying experiences, I can tell you!'' He chuckled, leaving no doubt as to the nature of those ''edifying'' experiences.

Amelia's cheeks colored even further, and Justin longed to box his brother's foolish ears for being such an improper dolt in front of her.

But Harry seemed quite oblivious to any distress or discomfort. He went on. ''I say, Justin! I'm going with some friends to the Golden Feather tonight. Why don't you come? It will be a proper welcome home.''

''And what might this Golden Feather be?'' Justin asked with careful casualness. He knew how much Harry would enjoy disapproval.

''It's a jolly place! My friends and I go there three or four times a week. It's a first-rate gaming hell, really top of the trees.''

''A gaming hell!'' Amelia cried. ''Harry, really.''

''Oh, Mother, it's not like that,'' Harry scoffed. ''You can't even really call it a hell. It's perfectly respectable. Members only allowed, and the members are all good *ton*. Nothing havey-cavey. Mrs. Archer wouldn't allow it.''

''Mrs. Archer?'' Justin said.

''She owns the place. Very lovely, but very mysterious. She always wears a mask.'' Harry's face softened as he spoke of this mysterious Mrs. Archer. ''You *should* come tonight, Justin. I have heard she means to sell the place soon, and it will never be the same without her.''

It sounded a perfectly dismal evening. Justin wanted only a bath, a brandy, and his bed. ''Harry, I hardly think . . .'' he began. Then he caught his mother's eye. She gave him a little nod.

She obviously thought that Harry could not get

into trouble with Justin watching his every move. And perhaps she was right.

So, even though his tired body was shrieking in protest, Justin nodded. "Thank you, Harry," he said. "I would like very much to go with you tonight."

Chapter Two

It was another busy evening at the Golden Feather.

Caroline stood alone in her small office, peering through her secret peephole at the large gaming room. Every chair was filled, every champagne glass glistened, and every table was piled with coins, notes, and jewels. Laughter and the sweet scent of the many flower arrangements floated through the air to her.

Even though the Season was winding to a close, the more daring of society still flocked to the Golden Feather, just as they had every night for four years now.

She gave a small smile. This was perfect. Perfect for one of her last nights in the gaming club. It would be a grand send-off, and no one in London would ever forget the mysterious Mrs. Archer.

Letting the little peephole cover slide into place, she turned back to her office and went over to the desk. The polished mahogany surface was covered with ledgers and papers, but she ignored them and reached for a small, neatly folded letter. She had read it a dozen times since it had arrived a week ago, but it still never failed to make her smile.

Phoebe was soon to finish her studies at Mrs.

Medlock's School for Young Ladies. Her excitement over her girlish plans seemed to spill from the carefully penned words. Caroline couldn't help but feel a bit excited herself. And not just for Phoebe, but for herself as well.

At long last, she was leaving the Golden Feather. The place had served its purpose well. She had a nice, tidy fortune tucked away, and stood to gain even more when she chose a buyer for the Golden Feather. She was a wealthy woman, and she and Phoebe would never have to worry about money again.

And if her soul had shriveled a little more each night as she strolled through the opulent rooms, watching fools lose their money, listening to lechers' suggestive whispers, it was worth it for that security.

Was it not?

Caroline carefully folded the letter and placed it in her locked drawer. Her only escape in these four years had been her annual holidays with Phoebe. Now they could be together all the time, be a true family again. *That* was worth anything, anything at all.

She had already arranged to rent a house for the summer, at the seaside resort of Wycombe-on-Sea, where they had sometimes gone with their parents as little girls. There she could rest at last and wash away the past years in the clean seawater. She and Phoebe could plan how best to introduce Phoebe to some kind of good society. Surely their parents' names still carried weight with someone. . . .

A knock sounded at the inner office door, interrupting these musings.

"Yes?" Caroline called.

"It's Mary, madam."

"Come in, Mary."

Mary was Caroline's maid, and had been ever since she had come to the Golden Feather. Once, in another life, she had been Caroline's nanny. She was the only other person who knew her true identity, and Caroline trusted her implicitly.

Mary bustled into the room, carrying a red wig, a black silk mask, and a small rosewood cosmetics box. "It's almost midnight, madam. They'll be expecting your grand appearance."

The tentative excitement and hope vanished before the prospect of the evening ahead. Caroline sighed. "Yes, of course."

Obviously sensing her melancholy, Mary patted her shoulder comfortingly. "It won't be long now, madam. In two weeks, maybe even less if that buyer comes through, we'll be gone from here."

"You are quite right, Mary. Not long now." Caroline rose from the desk and went around to the small, gilt-framed mirror on the wall. She took the red wig, fashioned into elaborate curls and decorated with ebony and crystal combs, and fitted it carefully over her own short, silvery-blond hair. Over it she tied the ribbons of the black silk mask that covered all her face except her mouth and lower jaw.

"Do you have the lip rouge?" she asked, making sure that no telltale blond strands showed beneath the red.

"Of course, madam." Mary brought the tiny enameled pot of rouge out from the cosmetics box and handed it to her.

Caroline used the little brush to paint her lips crimson, making them appear larger and richer than her usual pale rose bow. Then she slid glittering emerald drops into her earlobes and removed her shawl to reveal a low-cut, deep green satin gown. Long black gloves and high-heeled green satin shoes completed what she thought of as her "costume."

No one who ever encountered her as Mrs. Caroline Aldritch could possibly connect her to Mrs. Archer of the Golden Feather.

"All right, Mary," she said in a voice that seemed even deeper and lower. "I am ready to make my appearance."

Justin stood in the doorway between the dining room and the gaming room of the Golden Feather and looked about in growing boredom.

It was just like all the other gaming establishments he had frequented before he left for India. Fancier than most, perhaps, luxuriously appointed and full of fine flowers and champagne. And the people crowded around the tables were undoubtedly well dressed and well-bred, gentlemen in evening dress and ladies, some masked, in bright silks and jewels. But it was the same.

There was the same look on these people's faces, a mix of desperation and hope. The laughter had the same sharp edge. The same smell of liquor, cigar smoke, and perfume hung in the air.

What had he ever found so appealing in such places? It was appalling, especially after the brutal honesty and the shimmering skies of India. He wanted to run from it all, to breathe in fresh, clean air.

But once he had loved it all with a desperate excitement he saw now on his brother's face.

Harry sat at one of the card tables, avidly studying the hand he had just been dealt. A woman in a blue feathered mask sat beside him. She laid her kid-gloved hand on his arm and whispered something in his ear. Harry nodded and laughed, a sharp, brittle sound.

Justin noted the rather large pile of coins in front of his brother.

He frowned and would have started over to the table, but someone coming out of the dining room bumped into him. Champagne sloshed from the man's glass onto the marble floor, just missing Justin's shoe.

Justin turned around and came face-to-face with his old friend the Honorable Freddie Reed.

It had been only four years since Justin had seen him, on the morning of that fateful duel, but Freddie looked twenty years older. His eyes were bloodshot, underscored by bags and wrinkles. His skin was a grayish pallor, and his ample belly strained at his yellow brocade waistcoat.

Obviously, Freddie had continued on the pathway to dissipation he and Justin had started on so long ago. It was startling to realize that he himself might very well look like this if he had not gone out to India when he had.

Justin quickly concealed his astonishment behind a polite smile. "Freddie!" he said. "How are you, old man?"

"Eh?" Freddie squinted at him, then cried, "Justin! Dem me if it isn't old Justin Seward. Back from India, are you? Must have been very recently—you're as brown as a nut! Quite the pukka sahib." He laughed uproariously at his own weak witticism.

"Quite," Justin answered. "I only arrived in London today. I just came here to accompany Harry."

"Ah, yes. Young Harry. He's been following in his brother's footsteps, so I hear. I often see him about." Freddie turned to the woman at his side, a petite blonde in pink satin who was boldly unmasked. She was obviously as foxed as Freddie was, swaying unsteadily on her feet. "Meet Justin, m'dear. He used to be the boldest rogue in London. Now he's an old, respectable nabob, just back from India, and an earl to boot."

The woman giggled. "Pleased to meet'cha, I'm sure."

"Run along and wait for me at the faro table, sweet," Freddie told her. "I want to talk to Justin." The woman, sped on her way by a tap on the bottom from Freddie, left in a cloud of more giggles. Then Freddie turned back to Justin. "I am glad to see you again, Justin. Town's not been the same since old Larry Aldritch died and James Burne-Jones left. Not the same at all."

"Oh? Where did James go to?"

"Didn't you know? He left the day after your duel with Holmes, sent off to America by his father. I heard he married a rich widow in Boston." Freddie shook his head mournfully. "No, it hasn't been the same at all. But the Golden Feather is jolly good fun. Don't you think?"

Justin looked back out at the crowded gaming room. Harry was still at the same table with the woman in the feathered mask speaking to him quietly. "Indeed."

"I come here at least twice a week."

"The play is that good, is it?"

"Oh, yes. Champagne's not bad, either. And then there's Mrs. Archer." Freddie gave a blissful sigh.

"The owner?"

"Yes. She's a real beauty. At least I think she must be."

Was Freddie so drunk that he couldn't even see the woman straight, then? Justin laughed. "You mean you're not sure?"

"Well, she always wears a mask. But she has a beautiful voice. And a magnificent bosom. Though she is always so secretive; she will never give any man a second look, so they say. Ah, now see, you'll be able to judge for yourself."

A door at the top of a spiral staircase opened, and amid a sudden hush, a woman appeared on the landing there.

She was not especially tall, not above middling height, but she commanded the room just by standing still.

She wore a black silk mask that covered all her face except for her full red lips and an alabaster jawline. Her hair, a deep burgundy-red color, was piled atop her head in curls and whorls. The emeralds in her ears winked and dazzled in the light.

Mrs. Archer was very striking. And she did indeed have a magnificent bosom, its whiteness set off by the low bodice of her green satin gown.

Justin very much feared he was gaping, just as everyone else in the room was. But he couldn't seem to help himself; she was such a terribly striking sight.

"You see?" Freddie sighed. "Beautiful."

Then Mrs. Archer came down the stairs, her skirt held up daintily to reveal green heeled slippers and the tiniest amount of white silk stocking, and moved into the crowd.

Justin could see only the very top of her red head as she walked about, stopping to speak to various patrons and accept a glass of champagne from a footman.

He blinked and turned quickly away, feeling as if he were trapped in some bizarre, terribly attractive dream.

Chapter Three

Caroline had never seen him before. She was sure of it. If she had, she would have remembered him.

He stood in the doorway between the dining room and the gaming room, surveying the crowd with a look of almost-boredom on his face. He did not look contemptuous or disdainful, only as if he wished he were anywhere else.

And he was handsome. Very handsome indeed. His hair, a sun-streaked light brown, was a little longer than was strictly fashionable and brushed back in neat waves from his face. Unlike most of the men who came to the Golden Feather, he radiated good health and vitality. His skin was dark, as if he spent a good deal of time outdoors, and his tall, lean figure obviously had no need of corsets or of padding in his coats.

Beside all the other men who flocked around the gaming room, he stood out sharply, as a beacon of things that were honest and decent. Things like a fresh morning breeze, a brisk ride down a country lane, or a good laugh.

Things Caroline hadn't enjoyed for years.

She smiled wryly, mocking herself for such fanciful thoughts. A beacon of honesty, indeed! Here she had thought herself far beyond having her head turned by a pretty face. If he was here, he could scarcely be so decent as all that. No doubt he gambled terribly, just as Lawrence had. He was just a new patron, perhaps one who had recently come from the country.

Definitely one she should meet. After all, it was her job to make certain everyone who came to the Golden Feather enjoyed themselves.

Just her job.

Caroline made her way slowly across the room toward him, stopping to talk to people, to sip champagne, to check on the dealers at the various tables. All the while, she kept her eye on the stranger, where he stood talking to Lawrence's old friend Freddie Reed.

As she came closer, she felt a most unusual sensation fluttering in her stomach, tightening her throat. Was it . . . could it be nervousness? Nervousness at the thought of talking to a strange man?

Nonsense, she told herself briskly. It was only the champagne.

At last she reached them, and came to a halt to smile up at Freddie. "Good evening, Mr. Reed," she said. "So nice to see you here again."

Freddie blushed at this special attention, and stammered out, "G-good evening, M-Mrs. Archer! You are looking stunning, as always."

"Thank you very much, Mr. Reed." She glanced over at his companion, the handsome stranger, and tilted her head inquiringly.

"Oh!" said Freddie. "Mrs. Archer, I would like you to meet my friend, Lord Lyndon. He is just back from India and has never been to the Golden Feather before."

"How do you do, Mrs. Archer?" Lord Lyndon said, bowing over her outstretched hand. His fingers were warm through her thin glove, his grip steady and sure.

"Welcome to the Golden Feather, Lord Lyndon," she answered. "I do hope you are enjoying your first evening here."

"Of course," he said. "Who could help but enjoy themselves here? You have a lovely establishment, Mrs. Archer." But his eyes, a vivid sky blue in his sun-browned face, still looked bored and perfectly, blandly polite. His gaze slid ever so briefly over her shoulder before focusing on her again.

"Thank you, Lord Lyndon," she murmured, wondering what could possibly be so interesting behind her. Another woman, perhaps?

Her vanity was a bit piqued by this inattention. Unaccountably, she wanted this man's attention; she wanted his gaze to fill with admiration when he looked at her. Usually she disliked male attention and longed to turn away from their flattery, their long, suggestive glances.

"This may be Lyndon's first visit, but his brother is a regular patron," Freddie said, interrupting her jumbled thoughts.

Caroline turned to him in relief, away from Lord Lyndon's mesmerizing blue eyes. "Oh, yes? And who might that be?"

It was Lyndon who answered, in his deep, brandy-rich voice. "Mr. Harry Seward is my brother." He gestured with his champagne glass toward a table.

Caroline looked back to where he pointed. So that was what had caught his attention. His brother, Mr. Seward, was quite familiar to her. He came to

the Golden Feather several times a week, sometimes winning, more often losing. He was a bit of a
mischief maker, but she had never had any serious
trouble with him. Tonight he sat next to another
regular patron, a woman who called herself Mrs.
Scott, a bottle of champagne between them.

It was hard to believe that the feckless Mr. Seward was the brother of the serious, solemn man
who stood before her.

"We do see Mr. Seward often," she said.

"So I have heard," he answered softly. Caroline
had the distinct impression that he did not approve
of his brother's pastimes.

And that would mean he also disapproved of her.

Caroline glanced at Freddie and saw that his
glass was almost empty. "You need more champagne!" she said, half turning to summon a footman. Then she sensed Lord Lyndon's tall figure
stiffening beside her.

She followed the direction of his now-cold gaze
back to his brother's table. Harry had risen from
his chair to face another patron, a Lord Burleigh.
They were speaking together, if speaking was the
right word, their voices rising sharply. Harry's face
was red beneath his untidy shock of hair; his hands
were curled into fists at his sides. Mrs. Scott laid
her hand on his arm, trying to draw him away.

He shook her off impatiently and whipped back
around to face Lord Burleigh. A small crowd was
gathering, a hush settling over the room as people
noticed the brewing quarrel.

This was not good at all. There was nothing more
tiresome than a fight.

Caroline shifted her skirts so that she could better reach the small pistol tucked into her garter,

and looked about for the footmen who doubled as guards. Before she could find them, she felt Lord Lyndon's hand on her arm, moving her gently aside as started toward his brother.

"No, please, Lord Lyndon!" She caught his hand, stopping him from taking another step. "Let me handle this."

His eyes were now a stormy gray as he looked down at her. "He is my brother."

"I know. But I deal with this quite often, unfortunately. It will be easier if I speak to him."

Lyndon's jaw tightened, but he nodded shortly. "Damn," he said, "but I knew something like this would happen."

Caroline had just taken one step in Harry's direction when a high-pitched shout erupted from Lord Burleigh followed by a great crash as one of them, Harry or Burleigh, sent the card table toppling. Coins, cards, and champagne flew. There were shrieks and screams as everyone scrambled out of their way. Mrs. Scott sobbed hysterically, stamping her feet and shaking her champagne-splattered skirts.

"Oh, no," Caroline muttered. "This is just what I need on one of my last nights here." She lifted her skirts above her ankles and waded into the fray, closely followed by Lord Lyndon.

It took only seconds for a full-fledged brawl to form. Other people with grievances, seemingly inspired by Harry and Burleigh, broke into smaller fights. Harry himself had knocked Lord Burleigh down and was now planting him a sound facer in the nose. Mrs. Scott was deeply in hysterics.

Caroline picked up a heavy crystal vase, emptied the flowers onto the floor, and tossed the cold water onto the pair of them. It hardly made an impression, but it did thoroughly soak Mrs. Scott's gown, causing the woman to swoon.

It wasn't so good for Caroline's shoes, either.

Lyndon grabbed his brother by the coat collar and hauled him to his feet. Harry flailed helplessly for a moment but instantly stilled when Lyndon said, in tones of steely command, "Harold, you will cease this at once."

Harry quit wriggling and wiped at his bloodied nose with his coat sleeve. "He called Mrs. Scott a-a—"

"It doesn't matter what he said," Lyndon growled. "You should have taken your differences outside. There is no excuse whatsoever for causing a public scene in a lady's house."

Caroline stared at him, more startled by his words than she had been by the whole silly fight. A *lady's* house? She had never heard the Golden Feather—or herself—referred to in such a way.

She had the most unaccountable urge to give a pleased giggle.

"Now, apologize to Mrs. Archer, and we shall take our leave," Lyndon said, giving his brother a shake.

Harry glanced shyly at Caroline, then looked quickly away. "I am sorry, Mrs. Archer. What I did was completely unforgivable."

"Thank you, Mr. Seward," Caroline said, a bit bewildered. "You are forgiven."

"Freddie," Lyndon called to his friend, who was still drinking champagne in the doorway where they had left him, "would you please escort Harry, Mrs. Scott, and your—friend to the carriage and wait with them for me?"

"Of course," Freddie answered, coming forward to offer the sobbing and soaked Mrs. Scott his arm and taking firm hold of Harry with his other hand. "Glad to, Justin."

When they had gone, winding their way through the other, deliciously scandalized patrons, Lyndon turned back to Caroline. He smiled at her ruefully, and suddenly he no longer seemed the remote, polite, bored gentleman. He looked like a young boy, his hair rumpled and his cravat askew.

He swept his hair back off his brow, and said, "I, too, wish to apologize, Mrs. Archer. I hope that my brother does not always behave like this."

"Oh, no," she murmured, quite distracted by one wave of golden-brown hair that would not be tamed. It slid back down over his eye, only to be pushed away impatiently. "Mr. Seward is usually an utter lamb when he comes here."

"I am glad to hear it. I do want you to know that I intend to pay for any damages incurred this evening."

Caroline arched her brow, startled. That was a first. Usually when patrons owed her for damages, she had to threaten to set the Bow Street Runners on them in order to collect. And even that usually did not work.

"Well . . . thank you, Lord Lyndon," she said.

"I shall call on you tomorrow, then, if that would be convenient."

She would get to see him again tomorrow? Caroline's heart gave an unwilling little leap of expectation. She quickly reminded herself that this was strictly business, and said, "Yes, quite convenient. I live here at the Golden Feather, but you will have to knock at the side door."

"Very well." Lord Lyndon looked about at the shambles of the gaming room. The footmen had cleared out most of the quarreling patrons, but tables were upended, flowers and cards thick on the floor, and a couple of gilt chairs were broken. The elegant patrons of the "members only" Golden Feather had behaved as if they were in some pub in Whitechapel.

"Good evening, then, Mrs. Archer," he said. "If I dare call it a good evening."

Caroline laughed, suddenly exhausted and giddy. Perhaps it had not been a good evening, strictly speaking, but it had certainly been a different one. Not the usual evening in the gaming establishment at all. A handsome man and a brawl, all in one night. It was suddenly too much. She longed for her bed, for peaceful sleep.

"Yes. Good evening, Lord Lyndon."

He bowed over her hand again, then turned and left the chaotic room. Caroline watched his tall, dignified figure until the front door closed behind him. Then she knelt down with a sigh and began to pick up some of the rubbish on the floor.

Tomorrow. Lord Lyndon had promised to come back tomorrow.

She laughed again, as silly as a schoolgirl. Oh, this was bad. She should not be all calf eyed over some handsome lordship, not when a new, bright future lay before her. It could only ever lead to trouble.

She still couldn't help but laugh, just once more, as she thought of his lovely blue eyes.

"What were you thinking of, Harry?" Justin looked grimly across the darkened carriage to

where his brother huddled in the corner. They had
left Freddie and his lady friend and Mrs. Scott at
their respective houses, and were now alone.

And it was a long ride back to Seward House.

Harry pressed his handkerchief against his nose
and said sullenly, "Whatever do you mean, Justin?
You sound as if I just committed murder or
something!"

"And you sound as if this evening were just a
harmless lark."

"It was! Sort of. That old monkey Burleigh insulted Mrs. Scott. A gentleman would never let
such an insult stand."

"A gentleman would never get into a public fight
as you did, young pup. You made an absolute cake
of yourself in front of dozens of people."

"It was not worse than any number of the hums
you got into. At least I've never fought a duel. And
remember that opera dancer who actually came to
Seward House one night and threw rocks at the
windows and shouted for you for hours?"

Justin winced. He did indeed remember those
duels and that opera dancer. They had not been
his proudest moments. "I was once as young and
foolish as you, Harry. But I learned my lesson, and
I learned it the hard way. I had thought you might
be spared what I went through, that things could
be easier for you."

"So send me to India, then!" Harry burst out.
"How hard could it be there?"

"How hard could it be? You cannot even imagine, not living this sheltered English life. There are
snakes there as long as your leg, venomous enough
to fell ten horses with one strike. They curl up in
the garden and slip into the house by night; you

never know where they might be, where you could fall over them. There are natives who would just as soon kill you as look at you. Bandits who waylay travelers and strangle them with red scarves in the name of their goddess. Mosquitoes whine incessantly at night. The wet heat drains away all energy, all thought. And it is terribly lonely. There are no gaming hells, no racetracks, and very few Englishwomen."

Justin leaned his head back against the leather squabs as he fell silent, drained by his recitation, by the memory of all those things. India *had* been those things, true, and the thought of them made him shudder. But it also held its own strange enchantment. Especially the nights.

He recalled those nights, so warm, so full of the exotic scents of spices and sandalwood and strange flowers. Near his bungalow there had been the ruins of a Hindu temple, filled with bizarre, entrancing sculptures. He remembered how the moonlight would fall like pale, shimmering silk over this temple, how sitar music would echo off the ancient walls.

Mrs. Archer reminded him of India. She possessed that same strange, mysterious enchantment, the same exotic, fragrant allure. . . .

He shook his head fiercely to clear it of such thoughts. Women like Mrs. Archer, as lovely as she was, held no place in his life now. His focus had to be on his family and his proper place in life. He could not be distracted by lovely owners of gaming hells, or the siren song of India and all it stood for.

Harry, who had fallen silent after Justin's outburst, said, "Well, I thought all India teaches is how to be a stuffed-up old prig. You sound just

like Father, Justin. And you used to be such fun."
The words were meant to sound defiant, but they
came out instead sounding uncertain and very,
very young.

Harry was scared, Justin could tell. And so he
should be.

The carriage came to a halt outside Seward
House, and a footman hurried to open the door
and lower the steps.

"Go to bed now, Harry," Justin said, so unutter-
ably tired that he could scarce hold up his head. It
had been a very long night, and he was carrying
the weight of knowing how much he had let his
brother down. "We will discuss all this in the
morning."

Harry started to climb down from the carriage,
then paused, glancing back at Justin uncertainly.
"You . . . you won't tell Mother about this, will
you, Justin?"

Justin closed his eyes. Lord, had he ever felt this
weary before? "That remains to be seen, doesn't
it, Harry?"

Chapter Four

It was quite an unseasonably warm day. It was almost summer, but Caroline could not recall it being this warm until July at least. She opened the windows in her small office, letting in the noise from the street as well as what meager breeze there was. She even went so far as to take off her shoes and stockings. Deeply improper, of course, but who was there to see? Far better to be comfortable.

Caroline sat back down at her desk, where the accounts waited for her attention. She had received two good offers to buy the Golden Feather, and she wanted to be sure all her finances were in order before she accepted one and started to pack her trunks. She was in a great hurry to settle the sale and be gone, but somehow her mind would not stay on numbers today.

Her thoughts kept drifting away, to last night—and Lord Lyndon.

With a sigh, Caroline tucked her left foot under her right knee and absently rubbed at the thick scar on her ankle. She had had it for years; she and Lawrence had quarreled rather actively one night. He had broken a vase in his drunken rage, and she had accidentally tripped and cut her ankle deeply on the shards—and lost the baby she carried inside of her. It still itched on hot days or when her mind kept going over and over one subject without ceasing.

Caroline frowned. Why she would be so wrapped up in thoughts of Lord Lyndon she did not know. She had met dozens of men since Lawrence's death. Handsome men, rich men, witty men. Some of them, anyway, mixed among the ridiculous fools. Lord Lyndon was handsome, of course, and rather exotic with his India-dark skin and sad smile. And he was probably quite wealthy, if his large ruby stickpin, his fine carriage, and the way his brother threw money about were any indication. But really, how could he be different from any of those other men?

Oh, but he is, her secret, deepest inner voice whispered.

Caroline sighed again and stretched out her foot to prop it on the desk. Her blasted inner voice was right, as usual. Lyndon was different from the other men she had met, as different as a winter snowstorm from a hot summer afternoon. He had not been just rich and handsome; he had been kind.

He had spoken to her as if she were a person, a lady, who was due courtesy. He had not propositioned her or leered at her or peered ostentatiously down her bodice with a quizzing glass. Instead he apologized for his brother's bad behavior and offered to pay for the damages without any goading or arguing at all.

Most unusual.

Caroline reached out to rub at her scar. Very few men these past four years had bothered to speak politely to her. Manners, coupled with Lyndon's undeniable good looks, were a heady thing.

And that was surely all it was. Probably when he called today, *if* he called, his behavior would be very different. He would resort to typical maleness, would behave as all men did—in their own best interests.

She laid her hand flat against the scar.

Well, she could not afford to be distracted by any man, polite or not, no matter how handsome. She had to look after her sister, to rebuild their family, their lives. In a few short days, she would be respectable again, would go out into the world as Mrs. Caroline Aldritch again. She couldn't let a pair of handsome blue eyes threaten that, not even for a second.

Caroline swung her foot back to the floor and reached for the nearest ledger book. She had work to do, and nearly all the morning was already wasted.

But she had barely totaled up two columns of sums when a knock sounded at the door and Mary stuck her white-capped head inside. She, too, wore a half-mask, as she always did when admitting callers.

"There's a caller, madam," she said. "A *man*."

Despite her resolution of only moments ago, Caroline felt an excitement, an expectation, fluttering in her throat. It was he, Lyndon, it had to be!

She took a deep breath and closed the book. "Did he give his name, Mary?"

Mary handed her a card in reply.

Caroline looked down at the small, cream-colored square. In black print, it read, "Justin Seward, Earl of Lyndon."

Justin. So that was his name. Justin Seward. It sounded rather familiar, as if she had heard it somewhere before. But probably that was only because his brother, or someone else, must have mentioned it in passing. If he had been in India for years, surely he would not have been in the papers recently.

"I told him you never accept callers before luncheon," Mary sniffed, interrupting these ruminations. "But he said that he is expected."

"Indeed he is. His brother was the one who caused such a fuss last night, and he offered to pay for the damages," Caroline answered, carefully laying aside the card.

"Well! That *is* a first, madam."

"Yes, isn't it?" Caroline stood up and went to fetch the wig and mask that lay on a small table under the mirror. "Just give me five minutes, Mary, and then send him in."

After Mary left, Caroline went through the familiar motions of tucking her own cropped blond strands under the red wig, styled today in a simple upsweep. She tied on a blue satin mask and knelt down to retrieve her shoes from beneath the desk.

She debated putting her stockings back on, as any proper lady would, but then decided against it. It would take too much time, and Lord Lyndon would never notice if she remained seated behind the desk the whole time. She stuffed the flimsy bits of silk into a drawer and went to sit down and await the arrival of Lord Lyndon.

"Justin," she whispered to herself, then laughed at her own folly.

*   *   *

Justin followed the black-clad masked maid from the side entrance of the Golden Feather down a long, dim corridor to what he assumed would be a sitting room or office. He looked about in interest, never having been behind the scenes at a gaming house before. The private apartments were not at all the same as the public rooms, and not at all what he had expected. There was very little gilt or velvet, and no marble at all.

Instead, through half-open doors he could see cream-painted walls, old-fashioned furniture upholstered in pastel colors, piles of books, and well-executed landscapes in simple frames. Light, cream-and-gold striped draperies offered privacy from the busy city street but allowed the sun to filter into the small rooms.

It was a cool, pretty, inviting place, as elegant as anything his mother or one of her friends would have decorated. He could have stayed there happily all day.

Justin looked down at the long, pink-and-cream needlework rug beneath his boots.

All last night he had lain sleepless in his bed, thinking about the happenings at the Golden Feather and the mysterious Mrs. Archer. It seemed now that the conclusions he had reached at four in the morning were true. Mrs. Archer was a lady of some sort. Perhaps the ruined daughter of some country squire or a rich man's former mistress set up now in her own business.

Her voice had been educated, though pitched low and quiet, her gestures refined and polite. There was no coarseness about her, nothing that might be expected of a woman living the scandalous life of a gaming house keeper.

But, of course, those had all been impressions gathered in night's mysterious cloak. Darkness could hide a wealth of flaws and sins—as could a mask.

No doubt in the light of day, without the concealing scrap of silk, she would appear very different. Old, maybe, or pockmarked, or simply rude. She could not be what his fevered imaginings had suggested. That was impossible.

Just as he had thought it impossible she would wear a mask in the daytime. Then the maid ushered him into an office, and he saw that Mrs. Archer did indeed wear her concealing mask, even in this hot afternoon.

Her red hair was styled simply today, and her blue silk mask matched her very proper pale blue muslin day dress, but she still looked impossibly exotic in the spartan office.

Justin was seized with the desire, more intense than any desire he had ever known, to see what was beneath the mask.

It seemed that was not to happen, not today, anyway. Mrs. Archer rose behind the large, cluttered desk and held her hand out to him with a smile.

"Good afternoon, Lord Lyndon," she said, in the same low voice he remembered. "Won't you please be seated?" She gestured toward the straight-backed wooden chair situated across from her.

"Thank you, Mrs. Archer." Justin placed his hat and cane on the desk beside the pile of ledger books, and sat down. "I trust you have suffered no ill effects from last night's . . . incident?"

Mrs. Archer laughed. "Certainly not! It would take a great deal more than that little fight, I assure you. I am very glad to see you today, though, Lord Lyndon."

She was glad to see him? He felt an unwilling little frisson of excitement. "Are you indeed, Mrs. Archer?"

"Oh, yes. I have received two very good offers to buy this place, and I am sure I would have to lower my price if the necessary repairs are not made to the gaming room. Your offer of assistance does expedite things greatly."

"So you are really leaving the Golden Feather? My brother said something to that effect." Justin was unaccountably disappointed. Even if she stayed at the place for the next ten years, he could not come back here. Why would he care if she were there or not?

But he found he did care.

"Yes. I hope to be gone from here very soon."

"I am sure all your patrons must be desolate," he said, carefully impersonal.

She shrugged. "The new owner will keep things much the same. No one will notice the difference."

"I know that is not true. My brother calls you 'the incomparable Mrs. Archer,' and says you are the only reason so many flock here."

"Did he indeed? Your brother is very sweet. I trust he is not too ill today."

"He was still asleep when I left the house."

She nodded. "Sleep is the best thing for him. Perhaps when he wakes you could give him a glass of carrot juice mixed with one raw egg. It always helped my hus—" She broke off abruptly, her gaze falling back to the desk. "That is, I have heard many people swear by its efficacy after a night of overindulgence."

Had she been about to say her husband? Justin wondered, with a small jealous pang. Exactly what kind of man was Mr. Archer—or had he been—to deserve a wife like this one? "I wish I had known of such a cure in my younger days."

She smiled at him. "Were you a wild young man, Lord Lyndon?"

"I was terrible. Far worse than Harry."

"But India wrung it out of you, so to speak?"

"Indeed it did. It is hard to play the rake properly when one is laid low by humid heat and snakebite."

The satin of her mask wrinkled a bit as she frowned. "Were you bitten by a snake, then?"

"Twice. After that I learned to be wary. I was lucky to have a servant who knew all about how to treat such things, so I suffered no permanent ill effects."

Mrs. Archer propped her chin on her palm and said in a thoughtful voice, "India must have been very fascinating."

Justin looked at her and noticed for the first time that her eyes were brown. Deep and rich, like a cup of chocolate.

"Yes," he murmured. "Fascinating."

She stared back at him for a long moment. Then she seemed to recall where they were, *who* they were. She shook her head and sat up straight in her chair.

"Here is a list of all the damages," she said briskly, handing him a sheet of paper. "I estimated the cost of the repairs, which you will see here down at the bottom."

Justin dragged himself out of the enchanted cir-

cle of her eyes, her perfume, and forced himself to
look down at the paper. The neatly printed words
refused to come into focus.

He handed it back to her. Their fingers brushed
briefly, warmly. The gold of her wedding band, thin
and worn, glinted up at him.

That ring, a symbol of things respectable and
permanent, seemed to slap him across the face.

He meant to find a proper wife, to do honor by
his family. He should not be losing his senses over
a pretty gaming house owner!

"It all looks satisfactory," he said quietly.

"Good. If you would like to leave the money
with my maid, then, we shall be settled." She rose
again to her feet, and Justin followed.

She continued, in an oddly rushed and breathless
voice, "I am sure you must be very busy, Lord
Lyndon, so I won't detain you any longer." She
turned to walk around the edge of the desk. "I will
see you to the door. . . ."

Then suddenly half of her seemed shorter than
the other half. She gave a little squeak and tottered
a bit on her feet.

"Mrs. Archer!" Justin said, coming around the
desk and offering his hand to help her regain her
balance. One of her shoes, a high-heeled satin affair
with brocade ribbons, lay on its side just outside
the hem of her skirt. "Are you all right?"

"Oh, I am quite all right!" she said with an embarrassed little laugh. "I just forgot that I did not
lace my shoe properly when I put it back on
earlier."

"You had your shoes off?" Justin asked, not sure
he had heard her properly.

She shot him a haughty glance. "Of course. Doesn't everyone go about in bare feet on a hot day?"

He hardly dared to contradict her. Instead, he knelt down beside her and said, "Let me help you with your shoe, then."

She looked a bit reluctant, but then nodded and slid her foot from beneath her skirt.

He picked up the shoe, noticing with a start that she also did not believe in wearing stockings on a hot day. Terribly scandalous—and terribly attractive. He tried to ignore this, and slid the shoe onto her bare foot, holding the arch of it on his palm for one instant. It was slim and white in his hand, the bones as delicate as those of a small bird. Her toes wiggled, and she giggled a bit as his fingers slid over her sole.

He reached to tie the ribbons, and gasped. "You are injured!" he exclaimed.

Then he looked closer and saw that the gash on her ankle was an old one, not one she had just gotten. Thick, pale pink scar tissue arced across her creamy skin.

She had been badly cut at one time, but not today.

She tugged at her foot, trying to remove it from his grasp. He was almost thrown off his balance by this, and grasped her skirt to steady himself. " 'Tis an old injury," she said. "Not one to worry about."

"But what . . ."

He was interrupted when the office door opened and Mrs. Archer's maid came inside.

"Madam, I just wanted to see if—" She broke into a long scream when she saw him kneeling there, grasping Mrs. Archer's skirt. "What are you doing! Unhand her right now, you brute!"

The fragile-looking older woman grabbed a ledger book off the desk and commenced beating him about the head and shoulders with it. Her mask fell askew, but still she wielded the book.

It hurt like the very devil! Justin feared he would soon be knocked unconscious by the blows, and then what a scandal would ensue.

"Cease, woman!" he yelled, trying to grab at the book. "It is not what you think."

"Not what I think! I know your sort. You leave my lamb alone!"

"Mary, no!" Mrs. Archer reached down and hauled Justin to his feet. "I merely lost my balance, and Lord Lyndon was kind enough to help me. There was nothing improper at all."

"Oh?" Mary slowly lowered the book. "Truly, madam?"

"Truly, He has been the . . . the perfect gentleman."

"Well, in that case . . ." Mary placed the book back on the desk, straightened her cap on her graying brown curls, and her mask over her face and said, "Would you care for some tea, my lord?"

Chapter Five

"Did you conclude your business satisfactorily, then, dear?" Amelia glanced up from her embroidery and smiled as Justin came into the small, sunny sitting room.

"Quite satisfactorily." If one considered getting beaten about the head by an irate housemaid satisfactory. Justin almost laughed aloud at the memory of that chaotic scene. Then he almost groaned as the memory of another scene replaced it—that of holding Mrs. Archer's bare, elegant foot in his hand.

By Jove, but he had been too long without a woman if a naked foot could affect him so.

He sat down across from his mother and reached for a glass of lemonade, wishing it were something a good deal stronger. He needed it after the day he had had.

"There is cake, too," Amelia said.

"No, thank you, Mother. I stopped and had luncheon at the club. It's been years since I went there, but I found I am still on the membership books." He looked about the room again, thinking that it was too oddly quiet.

Then he realized why. Harry was nowhere in evidence.

Justin sighed and took another long sip of lemonade. His brother was probably off somewhere getting into trouble again. Justin had not thought it likely in the middle of the day, but a young man intent on mischief could find it at any time.

"I suppose Harry is out?" he said.

"Oh, no, indeed," Amelia answered. "He is still upstairs asleep."

"Asleep? In the middle of the afternoon?"

His mother gave a little, secretive smile as she plied her needle through the snowy linen. "I gave him a small dose of my old medicine. You remember, from back when the doctor said I had 'weak blood.' I have not taken the stuff since your father died, and I rarely give it to Harry. It is so difficult to give up once started, and it has made all the difference since I made myself give it up. But I felt he should stay home today. You will surely want to speak with him later."

Justin gave a doubtful snort. "My 'speaking to him' hardly seems to make any difference, Mother. The words simply go in one ear and out the other."

Amelia laughed. "Rather like someone else I once knew! I had also thought, though, that he might be more amenable to our summer plans if he had a good night's sleep."

"Oh? And what are our plans?" Justin reached for the crystal pitcher to pour out another glass of lemonade. "Are we off to Waring Castle, the ancestral pile?"

"We can go there if you like, of course. However, my friend Lady Bellweather called on me this morning, and she has given me a much better idea."

Lady Bellweather? She with the eligible daughter? Justin looked at his mother warily. "What sort of idea?"

"My dear, you sound as if I am about to suggest being boiled in oil! It is nothing onerous. Lady Bellweather is taking her children to Wycombe-on-Sea for the summer, and I thought how nice it would be to see that town again." Amelia smiled softly. "Your father and I went there once, when we were first married. Before any of you children came along. I thought it was truly lovely, a most amiable place. But your father preferred Waring or the hunting box in Scotland."

Justin saw the faraway glint in his mother's eyes and thought she must hold that long-ago trip to Wycombe-on-Sea in even greater esteem than she said. "So you never went back there?"

"Never. But we can go there now, if we so choose! I know it will not be the same as it was thirty years ago. Lady Bellweather goes there every year, though, and she says it is still delightful. There are assembly rooms and concerts, as well as the sea bathing. It is not as grand as Brighton, but I do think the fresh air would be so good for you and Harry."

"And for you, Mother?"

She laughed. "Perhaps! At least in Wycombe I shall know that my days of holidays spent standing about in bogs waiting for the grouse to fly, or whatever it was we were doing, are behind me now. What do you think, dear?"

Justin thought he would prefer the quiet of Waring to doing the pretty at some sea resort. But he had never seen his mother looking happier or more excited, and he didn't have the heart to take that away from her. "I think that Wycombe sounds a splendid idea."

Amelia leaped to her feet, her sewing falling unheeded to the floor, and rushed over to kiss his cheek. "Oh, my dear, you will not be sorry! We shall have such a grand summer. And just wait until you meet Miss Bellweather. She is truly lovely. Oh, I must go and start my packing! I hope I have the right clothes for the seaside."

With one last kiss, she hurried off, intent on her holiday.

Justin sat back in his chair, sipping at his lemonade, listening as his mother called for her maid. So the price he had to pay for his mother's happiness was meeting this Bellweather girl, was it?

Well, it was a price he was willing to pay. No doubt this girl was just the sort he should be thinking of marrying: well-born, well-bred, and well-versed in all the social graces of being a countess.

But somehow he could not erase the memory of a slim white foot, and brown eyes looking up at him.

Four days after Justin's visit to the Golden Feather, Caroline sat on her bedroom floor surrounded by open trunks and piles of books and belongings. The gaming house was sold, and she was at last truly going to put it all behind her.

She looked at her clothes, carefully stacked into piles. One contained her own dresses, modest muslins and silks meant to be packed and taken to Wycombe-on-Sea. The other was what she considered her "costumes," the brightly colored, daringly cut gowns she wore at the Golden Feather. They were to be given away, as she could never wear them at the seaside assembly rooms.

As she folded a stack of shawls, her gaze fell on a flash of emerald green. She reached out and pulled the gown from the bottom of the pile. The gown she had worn the night Lord Lyndon first came to the Golden Feather.

She spread the soft satin across her lap and examined the small watermarks along the hem. Perhaps she would keep just this one gown, as a memento.

A memento of a man she would never see again.

Caroline laughed and shook her head as she folded the gown. She was not generally prone to sentimentality; she could not afford to be. It must be the prospect of the sea air that was making her so maudlin today.

Beneath the pile of gowns was a silk-wrapped bundle. Caroline unwound it to find the miniature portrait of Lawrence. She held it carefully in the palm of her hand, studying the face painted there. It was almost like looking at the face of a stranger.

He had been gone for more than four years, and she had felt so many things for him in that time. Pity mostly, but anger, too. Anger for his weakness.

A weakness that, ironically, had given her the financial stability she craved, in his last gift of the Golden Feather.

Now all she could feel for him was gratitude and peace.

"Good-bye, Lawrence," she whispered as she re-wrapped the portrait and packed it away.

Mary came in then, freshly laundered linens in

her arms. "Have you decided what to take, madam?" she asked.

"I believe so. These trunks and those hatboxes can go. I do think, though, that I should visit a modiste before we leave. There are quite enough clothes for day, but a distinct scarcity of gowns suitable for the assembly rooms at Wycombe-on-Sea. I shall need a bathing costume, as well."

Mary gave a satisfied smile as she packed away the linens. "It will be very good to leave London."

"Indeed it will," Caroline agreed heartily. If she had her way, they would never see the blighted town again.

"I saw there was a letter from Miss Phoebe in this morning's post."

"Yes. She was so excited to receive the money I sent for new gowns. She also cannot wait to see us next week. I do believe she is very tired of Mrs. Medlock's."

"You can scarcely blame her, madam. She was at the school a whole year after her friends her own age left." Mary considered her longtime position as being sufficient excuse to always speak her mind.

"It could not be helped, Mary," Caroline answered quietly.

"I suppose not."

"Anyway, it has all worked out for the best! Now she is of just the right age to be married. I am sure we will meet a suitable young man in Wycombe. Someone calm and sober, not a wild young rake. Someone who can take proper care of her."

"And maybe a husband for you, too?"

Caroline looked up at Mary, startled. "A husband for me? No, indeed! I don't intend ever to marry again."

"What, never?"

"Never. Once was quite enough."

"But don't you ever wish for children? A family of your own? You may be twenty-eight years old, but there is still time."

Wish for children? Caroline looked back down at the trunk, staring unseeingly at the books stacked there. Once she *had* wanted children, very much. When she and Lawrence first married. She had grieved mightily at her miscarriage. Eventually, though, she had come to see their childless state as a blessing of sorts. Their lives together had been no place for an innocent babe.

And now . . . now it was out of the question.

"No," she said, too vehement even to her own ears. "I shall be an auntie to Phoebe's children one day, and that will be enough."

"But if you should meet someone you really liked . . . ," Mary persisted.

Someone with bright blue eyes and a wry, crooked smile? "I won't meet anyone again," she insisted. "Besides, we are not going to Wycombe to meet someone for me. We are going to find someone suitable for Phoebe."

Chapter Six

"Caro! Oh, Caro, you are here at last! I've been waiting hours and hours."

Caroline had just stepped down from the carriage outside Mrs. Medlock's School when Phoebe came flying down the front steps and flung herself into Caroline's open arms.

"Silly Phoebe!" Caroline laughed, holding her sister close. "I told you we would surely not arrive before teatime at the earliest."

"Tea was half an hour ago. Though I'm sure Mrs. Medlock would have a fresh pot made, if you like."

"Tea would be lovely. But first I want to look at you." Caroline held her sister out at arm's length for an inspection.

"Have I grown, then?" Phoebe preened a bit, turning her head from side to side so that her curls danced. "Am I taller than when you saw me last autumn?"

Phoebe was not taller, but she did seem somehow older than she had on that last visit. Then her hair had been down, a riot of golden curls to her waist. She had worn the school uniform and giggled and whispered with her friends as any immature girl would.

Today her hair was pinned in a fashionable knot atop her head, and she was obviously trying very hard to contain her natural exuberance and behave like a lady. Her hands were clasped tightly in front of her as she bounced slightly on her feet. She was a bit taller than Caroline, and in Caroline's sisterly opinion anyway, much prettier, with soft violet-blue eyes and pink-and-white skin.

She no longer looked like the baby sister who would follow Caroline all around their childhood home. She looked like a young lady.

A young lady with strange tastes in clothing.

Caroline gazed speechless at Phoebe's ensemble. When she had sent money for new clothes, Caroline had pictured sprigged muslin day dresses and pastel ball gowns. Today Phoebe wore a gown of bright orange lightweight wool, trimmed *à la militaire* with copious gold braid and frog fastenings. A gold lace ruff framed her pretty face, and more lace peeked out at the cuffs.

"Oh, Phoebe," Caroline said quietly, "you look . . . very dashing."

"Do you like it?" Phoebe spun about happily. "I was quite in alt when you said I might have some new gowns. The dressmaker in the village has some lovely fashion plates from London, and she made up such gowns for me. Just wait until you see them! I am sure there can be nothing so fine in Town."

"I am sure not."

Phoebe looked closely at Caroline's own pale gray carriage dress and matching plain bonnet. "Perhaps she could make up something for you, Caro."

Heaven forbid. "Well, dear, I am sure we won't

have the time. We must leave tomorrow, you know, for Wycombe-on-Sea."

"I cannot wait! I have told all the girls about what adventures we shall have. They are quite envious, I assure you. But you must come inside now and have some tea, for you must be vastly tired after your journey! Did Mary come with you?"

"She stayed at the inn with the luggage. You know how she is; she does not trust anyone."

"I can scarcely wait to see her! I'm sure she won't recognize me again."

"I am sure she won't."

Mrs. Medlock appeared then in the doorway, a tall, stern-looking woman in rustling black silk.

"Miss Lane," she said, "I am sure your sister would like something to drink after her journey. It is very warm out here to be kept standing about."

Phoebe smiled at her, dimples flashing prettily. "Of course, Mrs. Medlock."

"Why don't you go ask the maids to lay out the tea again, while I show Mrs. Aldritch where she might refresh herself."

"Oh, yes! I will see if there are any lemon cakes left, since they are your special favorites, Caro." Phoebe kissed Caroline's cheek once more and dashed off to find the dessert, her orange skirts held up to reveal gold-colored stockings and slippers.

"If you would care to follow me, Mrs. Aldritch," Mrs. Medlock said, turning back into the school in Phoebe's wake.

As Caroline followed the headmistress up a winding staircase and along a dim corridor, Mrs. Medlock said, "Miss Lane is very excited about her seaside holiday, Mrs. Aldritch."

"I am rather excited myself," Caroline answered. "It feels I have waited a very long time for her to finish her studies and be ready to make her bow in the world."

"Yes." Mrs. Medlock opened a door and ushered her into a small sitting room, where a basin, towels, and soap were laid out. "You will probably be considering a match for her soon."

"Very likely, if someone suitable appears."

Mrs. Medlock nodded. "She is a very pretty girl, Mrs. Aldritch. I am certain she will have no lack of suitors. But I feel I must also tell you that Miss Lane is one my most, er, *exuberant* students. I realize this is hardly my place to say, but . . ." Her voice faded in hesitation.

Caroline removed her bonnet to look closer at Mrs. Medlock. What exactly was the woman trying to say? "Please, Mrs. Medlock, do go on."

"It is only that I am so fond of your sister, Mrs. Aldritch. I would hate to see any . . . difficulties befall her. And I know that these seaside places are full of all sorts of people, including gentlemen whose behavior is less than respectable. Miss Lane has such an *impulsive* nature."

"So you are urging me to keep a strict eye on her, is that it, Mrs. Medlock?"

The headmistress nodded in relief. "Yes. That is all. Just be vigilant, Mrs. Aldritch. Now, I will leave you to freshen up. One of the maids will show you to the drawing room when you are ready."

With Mrs. Medlock gone, Caroline turned back thoughtfully to the basin of water. Mrs. Medlock, who had always been so proper and reserved on the few times they had met in the past, was urging her to be "vigilant" about Phoebe? What was going on?

Caroline frowned at her reflection in the small mirror above the basin. She had thought it would be so easy to be a chaperon and mother figure. They would go to Wycombe, Phoebe would meet some sober young vicar or squire, and she would marry him and be secure and cozy for the rest of her life.

Oh, Caroline knew that Phoebe was rather high-spirited, as all young girls were. There had been occasional letters from Mrs. Medlock about some small prank or other Phoebe and her friends had undertaken. But those had been ages ago. Phoebe was seventeen now, a young lady of an age to settle down.

Caroline thought very carefully now about Mrs. Medlock's words. She had been so very certain that Phoebe would be eager to listen to her counsel, to meet *nice* young men. She was so intent on making certain that Phoebe did not make *her* past blunders that perhaps she had not seen the obvious.

That perhaps Phoebe was exactly like Caroline was at her age, heedless and romantic, ripe for making mistakes.

At least Mrs. Medlock had seen fit to warn her.

"I *will* be vigilant," Caroline whispered fiercely. "Phoebe will not end up with another Lawrence, that I promise."

Phoebe watched Caroline carefully across the tea table, where she sat making polite conversation with Mrs. Medlock and the music instructor. Her sister was not exactly as she had remembered.

Phoebe always thought of Caroline as being elegant and sophisticated, as indeed she was, though rather plain in her dress for Phoebe's taste. From her childhood, she remembered her sister as being fun, with a ready smile and a merry laugh. She had always been ready for any lark.

The Caroline who sat across from her now, the Caroline she had known for the past few years, always seemed rather, well, worried. Quiet and intense, as if she always had some deep worry lurking in her mind.

Phoebe smiled secretly behind her teacup. Well, *she* would soon have her sister smiling again. And laughing and dancing and wearing bright, daring colors. Making merry was what Phoebe did best; all her friends agreed that she was the very best at coming up with pranks to pull on Mrs. Medlock. And Wycombe-on-Sea sounded like it could be very merry indeed. At least compared with this school.

The sort of place where a determined girl could get up to some grand schemes.

"Why must we go to a sea resort, of all places?" Harry whined for the tenth time in as many minutes. "There will be no one but old ladies and invalids there. If we *have* to go to the sea, we could at least have gone to Brighton."

Justin frowned at his brother. They had been trapped together in the carriage for hours, and Justin had had about all he could take of Harry's complaints. If he had to hear one more, he would surely toss Harry out of the carriage on his gold satin-covered backside.

Their mother, though, didn't appear to notice the squabbling at all. She watched the landscape pass by out the window, humming a cheerful little tune under her breath.

"We are not going to Brighton, Harry," Justin said through gritted teeth, "because there are too many opportunities for you to get into trouble there, with the Prince Regent and his cronies in residence."

Harry crossed his arms over his puce-and-gold striped waistcoat. "I promised you I would not associate with the Carlton House set if we went to Brighton! I would have behaved myself."

Justin snorted in disbelief.

"I would have! There was absolutely no reason for you to drag me off to some old watering place full of matrons and doddering old colonels looking to cure their gout. I would wager there is not a single place where one could get a decent game of cards in the whole town. And no pretty girls, either."

"Harry . . . ," Justin warned, looking at their mother to gauge her reaction to his rude words.

Amelia just laughed. "I do believe you would lose that wager, Harry dear. I gave your father fits the last time we were here, I lost so much at piquet and vingt-et-un." She laughed again, brightly. "Yes, indeed, *fits!*"

Harry looked marginally more interested, but persisted in his sulks. "That was thirty years ago, Mother."

"Things could not have changed that much," Amelia replied, unfazed. "And as for pretty girls, I am sure there will be no shortage of them. Lady Bellweather alone has three daughters, though I fear the youngest two are far from marriageable age. But the eldest will surely gather a crowd of young people around her. So there will be no lack of activities for you, Harry dear, and do stop pouting. It ruins your handsome face and makes you look quite old and crabbed."

"No!" Harry cried, horrified.

Amelia smiled serenely and went back to looking out the window.

Justin, amazed at the sudden silence, took out his book and opened it to where he had left off. But he could not concentrate on the words at all.

He kept seeing red hair and small white feet, kept hearing the low, soft sound of a woman's voice. Mrs. Archer's voice. Without the distraction of Harry's whining, his thoughts constantly went back to the dark-eyed woman.

It was absolutely fruitless, of course, all this ruminating on who she might be, what she might look like beneath her mask. He was not looking for a mistress, and even if he were she was far away.

One thing was certain—he would surely never see her again.

He laughed softly and went back to his book. Mrs. Archer could only be a small, bright memory now, a memory of a woman he had scarcely known but who had interested him, drawn him in.

He could only hope that Miss Bellweather, or someone like her, would be half as intriguing.

Chapter Seven

"Oh, Caro, is it not the loveliest house you have ever seen in your life!" Phoebe ran from room to room in their new cottage, throwing open all the window casements to let the fresh sea air in. "And we have such a grand view of the water. It is just like the Castle Tallarico."

Caroline removed her bonnet and placed it next to her gloves and reticule on a small table. She was quite tired from their journey, but she couldn't help smiling at Phoebe's whirlwind of enthusiasm. The girl had chatted practically nonstop for the whole trip and showed no signs of stopping now that they had arrived in Wycombe. "Castle Tallarico?" she asked.

"From *Contessa Maria's Secret*. Have you not read it?"

"I fear I have not."

"Oh, but you simply must! It is the finest book ever written, I am sure. Contessa Maria comes to live at Castle Tallarico, which is exactly like this place. Well, almost. It is a great, crumbling, medieval stone castle, and this is a red brick cottage. But there is an ocean crashing against cliffs below, and there are secrets and a sinister housemaid and a secretive but fatally attractive prince who is the hero." Phoebe turned wide eyes to her sister. "Caro! Do you think we shall meet a fatally attractive prince here? Perhaps even in that grand house next door!"

Fatally attractive? Lord Lyndon's smile flashed in Caroline's mind, as it had so often, *too* often, in the past days. She pushed it back, reminding herself one more time that she would never meet Lyndon again. "I doubt it, dearest. Though I am sure we will meet many nice young men."

"Nice!" Phoebe wrinkled her nose in disgust. "That makes them sound like spaniels."

"There is nothing wrong with being nice," Caroline chided. "It is far better than being . . . fatally attractive."

Phoebe looked unconvinced. But she just shrugged and went back to peering out the window. "Look, there are people out walking along the shore! Can we go down there, Caro?"

Caroline shook her head. "Not today. It grows late. Perhaps we can go for a stroll tomorrow, or even bathing. Would you like that?"

"Above all things!" Phoebe spun away from the window to give Caroline an impulsive hug. "Are you quite all right, Caro? You look so pale."

"I am just tired, dearest. The journey was such a long one."

"Indeed it was! You should not sit in one place for so long when you are older. You stay here, and I will go see how Mary and the new cook are getting along for supper. Shall I bring you some tea, too?"

Caroline laughed at that "older" comment. "Yes,

please. A cup of good, strong tea sounds just what I need to warm my ancient bones."

After Phoebe rushed out of the room in a flurry of bright pink skirts, Caroline settled herself in a chair by the window. She looked out at the stretch of sandy shore in the not-too-far distance, watching the few people who walked there soaking up the last of the warm afternoon before they went off to their evening's festivities.

Festivities she and Phoebe would soon have to find a way to gain entrance to.

Tomorrow she would look about the town, see who was in residence. Surely there would be someone here who would remember her family, the Lanes; they had summered here so often when she was a child. Someone who would not remember the mild scandal of her elopement with Lawrence Aldritch. Someone who would welcome them. They only had to pay for their tickets to go to the assembly rooms, of course, but that would do them no good without someone to introduce them.

She looked away from the window, and her gaze fell on Phoebe's bonnet, abandoned on a settee. Its pink and gold and green feathers fluttered in the breeze from the open window.

Caroline sighed. Someone would have to give Phoebe some fashion advice, as well.

There was a clatter of carriage wheels in the street below, the last street before the sandy shore sloped down into the sea. They stopped in front of the house next door.

Caroline peered back out, curious to see who had taken the large, white stone structure.

A footman opened the carriage door, and a loud,

querulous voice floated out, ". . . didn't say we
would be in such a pokey little place! I vow my
old governess must live in a larger house. I told
you we should have gone to Brighton!"

A woman's sweet, barely audible voice answered,
"Your father and I stayed in this exact same house.
It is much larger than it appears, I promise, and it
is right on the water. . . ."

One booted foot just emerged from the carriage
when Phoebe reappeared, carrying a large tea tray.
Caroline turned from the window, closing the case-
ment firmly behind her. She didn't want Phoebe to
know yet that their neighbors, far from being "fatally attractive" royalty, were quarrelsome snobs
who thought their great mansion too small.

The next day was bright and warm, perfect for
strolling along the promenade that ran alongside
the shore. Perfect for seeing and being seen.

Caroline just wished that Phoebe chose to be
seen in something other than a purple-and-yellow
striped muslin walking dress and purple spencer.

More than one passing matron looked at Phoebe
with raised brows, then, more often than not, would
turn their gaze to Caroline in a most accusing manner. Almost as if they were blaming *her* for the
young woman's attire!

Caroline just smiled, sighed inwardly, and fought
the urge to dare one of those old hens to try to
change Phoebe's mind. She had already taken her
sister to see three dressmakers, had pointed out
how attractive pale pink and cream were next to
golden curls and violet eyes.

Phoebe had just shaken her head, pulled out

bolts of bright blue and sunburst yellow, and said how lovely *they* were for Caroline's dark eyes. She shunned chipped-straw bonnets and pretty pale blue trims. But she begged for a wide-brimmed hat trimmed with yards of red tulle veiling and numerous pink roses.

Caroline sighed again. Now she knew what her mother had meant when, long ago, she had said that one day Caroline would have a daughter just like herself, and then she would know what it felt like.

Phoebe, though, was oblivious to all this. She hurried ahead on the promenade, practically skipping in enthusiasm. She swung her new hatbox blithely by its ribbons and smiled at everyone she passed.

Mary came up beside Caroline, carrying the extra parcels of ribbons and slippers, puffing slightly from the exercise. "I did think, madam, that you said a seaside holiday would be restful after that den of vice in London."

Caroline laughed. "Are you not rested, then, Mary?"

Mary looked ahead to where Phoebe was chasing after some seagulls, and said, "Not just at present."

"Things will settle soon, I am sure. It's just that she is in a new place, and everything is so exciting. She can't stay this energetic forever."

"Hmph. If you say so, madam."

"I do say so. Now, Mary dear, if we just—"

"Excuse me," a woman's soft voice said from behind Caroline, interrupting her words.

Caroline turned and saw a small, slender, pretty older woman. She was obviously Quality, with her soft gray walking dress and fine pearl necklace and earrings. Her only slightly faded blue eyes were hesitant but intent as she looked at Caroline.

"Yes?" Caroline said. "Oh, are we blocking the walkway? I am so sorry!"

"No, not at all. It is just . . . Oh, this is terribly bad-mannered of me to just come along and speak to you like this! But I had to know if you were perhaps related to Margery Elliston."

Caroline looked closer at the woman, startled. "She was my mother."

The woman smiled in satisfaction. "I knew it! You look so very much like her. We were schoolmates, you see, back when I was just Miss Amelia Petersham. What larks we did have together then!" The woman laughed softly. "But I don't mean to keep you with my sentimental rambling, Miss . . ."

"Mrs. Caroline Aldritch," Caroline answered with a smile of her own. This was just what she had been hoping for, someone who remembered her family. And this Amelia Petersham, or whatever her name was now, seemed so very kind. "You are not keeping me at all. I am always happy to meet a friend of my mother's."

"Oh, the stories I could tell you about her! I was so saddened when I heard of her passing. But have you been in Wycombe very long? Are you here with your husband?"

"I fear my husband has also passed away, several years ago."

The woman nodded in sad sympathy. "I am sorry. Widowhood can be so very difficult, as I well know. I trust you are not alone, though?"

"I am here with my sister, Miss Phoebe Lane, who you see just there." Caroline caught Phoebe's eye where she had wandered rather far afield and motioned her to come back closer.

"I am here with my family, as well, my two sons and a friend and her daughters. They are taking tea at that shop, and I fear I abandoned them most rudely. But I saw you out the window, and I simply had to come and see if you had known Margery." She laughed and pressed one gray-gloved hand to her throat in obvious embarrassment. "And now I am being rude again, not introducing myself to you! I am Lady Lyndon; well, I suppose I am the *Dowager* Lady Lyndon now."

Lyndon? Her name was Lyndon? Caroline's breath seemed to stop in her throat, choking her. She stepped back from the woman, staring at her, trying to see some resemblance to *him* in her pretty face.

Surely she could not be related to the Lord Lyndon, Justin, who had come to the Golden Feather? That would simply be too much coincidence, too much like one of Phoebe's beloved silly novels. But there could not be two Lord Lyndons in England.

Oh, what if he was here! How terrible that would be.

But how wonderful, her traitorous mind whispered, if she *did* see him again . . .

"Mrs. Aldritch?" Lady Lyndon said, clearly alarmed. "Are you quite all right? You look rather faint."

"It is just the sun, Lady Lyndon," Caroline managed to gasp.

"Yes, it is rather warm to be standing about. Won't you join us in the tea shop?"

Phoebe came up to them just in time to hear

this. Even though she could have no idea who this woman was her sister was conversing with, she said with great enthusiasm, "A tea shop? Oh, yes, Caro, let's! I am quite famished."

Go to the tea shop, where no doubt this woman's sons, both of whom had met her as Mrs. Archer, were waiting? Caroline did not think that a wise idea. She had to collect her scattered thoughts before she met Lord Lyndon again. "We would not want to intrude," she said.

"Of course you would not be intruding!" Lady Lyndon protested. "Ah, here come my sons now."

Caroline pressed her gloved hand to her suddenly heaving stomach. What if this truly was *him*? What if he recognized her and told all the world the truth about her past?

But a part of her, a part she scarcely dared acknowledge, hoped that it was he.

She turned around and pressed her hand even tighter to her stomach. It *was* he. Justin.

His hair glinted almost a gold in the sunlight, and the lines about his vivid blue eyes deepened as he smiled at his mother. His gaze flickered over Caroline, too, in curiosity.

She reached up, unconsciously trying to tug the wide brim of her bonnet forward even farther, so she could hide beneath it.

Next to her, Phoebe had gone suddenly still, ceasing to bounce on her feet for the first time all day. "Oh, Caro," she whispered, "is he not the handsomest man you ever saw! He should be in a novel."

Caroline looked at her sister, horrified. Phoebe, attracted to Justin? What a nightmare. How could she possibly like him when he was *hers,* Caroline's?

She was even more horrified by that quick, flashing thought. Of course he was not hers; he never could be.

But he could not belong to Phoebe, either. The very thought was absurd!

"Phoebe," she whispered back, "he is above ten years older than you!"

"How can he be? I declare he must be only one-and-twenty at the most."

Then Caroline saw that in her haste to jump to ridiculous conclusions, she had missed the fact that Phoebe was not looking at Justin at all. Her gaze was focused past him, on the man who followed him.

A man in an orange brocade waistcoat and pea-green coat.

Harry Seward.

"Is he not a vision?" Phoebe sighed.

Caroline groaned and closed her eyes against the "vision." Oh, why could the ground not just open up and swallow her whole!

Chapter Eight

"Justin! Have you ever seen such an angel of perfection before?" Harry whispered. He stopped moving forward in midstride and stood frozen as a block of marble, his eyes wide and staring.

Justin, too, looked at the woman who stood talking to their mother and decided that for once he had to agree with his brother's taste. She was as close to an "angel of perfection" as he had seen since . . .

Well, since his afternoon in Mrs. Archer's office. Not that this lady resembled Mrs. Archer in any way. She was dressed quietly but stylishly in a walking dress of pale yellow muslin and a yellow and white bonnet. Even though her face was half in shadow from that bonnet's wide brim, he could see a small, straight nose, aristocratic cheekbones, and soft, silvery blond hair.

Yes, she was lovely. He would have thought her too subtle for Harry's taste, though.

He glanced at his brother, oddly irritated that Harry had seen her first. "She's not exactly in your style, is she?"

"What are you talking about?" Harry shot back. "She is exactly in my style! Only a true paragon of fashion could have chosen that sublime shade of purple."

Only then could Justin tear his gaze away from the lady in yellow to the girl who stood beside her.

Now, *she* truly was in Harry's style.

She had very pretty golden curls and was obviously young and high-spirited. But she wore a gown that was much too old for her, of bright purple-and-yellow striped muslin topped with a purple braid-trimmed spencer. On her head perched a tall-crowned purple hat ornamented with a band of gold lace. If Justin had been in the habit of wearing a quzzing glass, he would have been groping for it.

"She seems to know Mother, too," Harry said eagerly. "Come on, let's see if she'll introduce us." He came unfrozen then and hurried forward, all his fashionable weariness and whining forgotten in his rush to meet the "paragon of fashion."

Justin followed, more than a little curious himself to meet these new arrivals.

Especially the lady in yellow.

"There you are, my dears," his mother said. "Do come and meet my new acquaintances, Mrs. Aldritch and her sister, Miss Lane. These are my two sons, Lord Lyndon and Mr. Harry Seward."

The lady in yellow looked at them rather coolly, her fair face expressionless as a mask. "How do you do, Lord Lyndon, Mr. Seward?" she said quietly.

Justin had the distinct impression that she was quite underwhelmed to make their acquaintance. As she tilted up her chin a bit, he wondered if perhaps he had forgotten to bathe that morning.

The other lady showed no such reservations. She seemed to bounce on her feet and smiled up at them brightly. "How do you do!" she said, her pretty violet-blue gaze fastening on Harry.

"How do *you* do, Miss Lane?" Harry said, then added hastily, "And you, Mrs. Aldritch. Dashed glad to meet you."

Miss Lane giggled, and Mrs. Aldritch laid her hand on her sister's purple-covered arm, stilling some of that dizzying bouncing.

Justin suddenly realized that he was staring, quite rudely, and said quickly, "Have you been in Wycombe very long, Mrs. Aldritch?"

"Not at all," she answered, still very quiet. She ducked her chin back into the shadow of her bonnet, giving the impression of great shyness or reserve. A reserve he longed to pique. "We only arrived yesterday, and your mother is our first acquaintance here."

"They are the daughters of an old friend of mine," Amelia said happily. "Isn't that the most marvelous coincidence?"

"Marvelous," Justin echoed, watching the quiet Mrs. Aldritch.

"And now you must join me in persuading them to come back to the tea shop with us and meet the Bellweathers," Amelia continued.

Justin almost groaned aloud. The Bellweathers! How could he have forgotten them not five minutes out of their company? He was meant to be paying special attention to Miss Sarah Bellweather.

"Oh, you must!" Harry burst out. "You must join us, I mean. They have the most excellent strawberries."

"I adore strawberries!" Miss Lane said, with another little bounce for enthusiastic emphasis. She looked to her sister inquiringly. Only when Mrs.

Aldritch gave a small nod did she bounce forward to take Harry's arm.

He led her toward the tea shop, both of them chattering happily away. About fashion, no doubt.

"Well, then, Mother. Mrs. Aldritch," Justin said, offering an arm to each of the ladies. "Shall we join them before they devour all the strawberries?"

"And where is your family *from,* Mrs. Aldritch?" Lady Bellweather, a rather buxom matron with suspiciously dark hair arranged in girlish curls about her creased face, sounded as if she strongly suspected Caroline's family came from a cave somewhere. Her eyes were narrowed as she peered at Caroline over her large plate of cake.

Caroline took a slow sip of her tea, acutely conscious of Lord Lyndon seated beside her at the crowded table. The way his shoulder almost, but not quite, brushed against her made it very difficult to concentrate on Lady Bellweather's prying questions. Or indeed on anything at all.

She leaned away from him a bit and carefully placed her cup and saucer back on the table. "My sister and I grew up in Devonshire, Lady Bellweather. Our mother, as you know, was Miss Margery Elliston, and our father was Sir William Lane."

"And you say you were married?" Lady Bellweather's tone implied that that claim was also highly suspect.

Caroline almost laughed. If only Lady Bellweather knew what she had really been doing for the last few years! The woman would surely faint dead away if she heard of the Golden Feather, a not wholly undesirable thought. "Indeed I was, though my husband, Mr. Lawrence Aldritch, has been gone for many years."

"Larry Aldritch?" Lyndon said suddenly. "You were married to Larry Aldritch?"

Caroline, Lady Bellweather, and Lady Lyndon all looked at him in surprise. He had been very quiet ever since they sat down.

Caroline was more than surprised; she was dismayed. He had known Lawrence, had known him well enough to call him Larry? Only his closest cronies, the ones he went drinking and gaming with, had called him by that nickname. But how could that be? Lord Lyndon seemed such a gentleman, not at all like Lawrence's rackety friends.

Wasn't he?

Caroline looked at him closely for the first time since they met on the promenade, searching for signs of dissipation beneath that handsome, pleasant veneer.

Then she realized that now he could see her fully, too, with her face turned to him and her bonnet's brim no longer in the way. He watched her steadily, seriously, a bit curiously. Not only that, but an awkward silence had fallen at the table. Even the two littlest Bellweather girls stopped their chatter to watch Caroline's dumbfounded reaction to his question.

Lady Bellweather gave a smug little smile, as if she were certain there was some scandal attached to this "Larry" Aldritch.

Caroline looked away, and said, "Some people called him Larry, yes. Did you perhaps know him, Lord Lyndon?"

"Yes. A long time ago, before I went out to

India. May I offer my belated condolences on his passing, Mrs. Aldritch?"

"Thank you," Caroline answered, unsure what else she should say. She wanted to ask what his friendship with Lawrence had been like, what sort of trouble they had gotten into together. If he had been one of the spoiled young noblemen who encouraged Lawrence to gamble far more than he could afford to lose.

Her hands clenched in her lap, hidden by the tablecloth. She didn't want to believe that of Lord Lyndon! She *wouldn't* believe it. His behavior the night he came to the Golden Feather with his brother had not been that of a wastrel.

She carefully looked up at him again and gave him a small smile. "Perhaps you could tell me more of your acquaintance with my husband, Lord Lyndon. One day."

He smiled at her warmly in return. "I should like that, Mrs. Aldritch."

Lady Bellweather put her cake plate down on the table with a loud rattle. "I have never heard of anyone named Aldritch," she pronounced.

"Oh, Mother, please," the eldest Bellweather girl, Sarah, said. She tossed back her dark brown curls impatiently. "We live right next to old Miss Dorothy Aldritch in Grosvenor Square. Wasn't her nephew named Lawrence?"

Phoebe, who had been talking with Sarah ever since they sat down, giggled. The two younger Bellweathers gasped.

Lady Bellweather turned a deep burgundy-purple.

And Caroline, not for the first time that strange afternoon, had no idea what to say. Her mind was too full for any more thoughts just at present. She pressed her fingertips to her aching temples.

It was Lady Lyndon who saved the day. "Well, it does grow rather late, I fear," she said cheerfully. "I do hope, Mrs. Aldritch, that you and your sister can come to my little card party tomorrow evening? There will be a supper before, and it should be quite amusing."

Caroline looked around at all the people gathered about the tea table. Lady Bellweather's expression was most disgruntled as she frowned at her friend. Sarah and Phoebe were whispering together intently, while Harry stared, wide-eyed, at Phoebe. Lady Lyndon smiled expectantly.

And Lord Lyndon watched her intently, waiting for her answer.

Her headache intensified, but she smiled and said, "Of course, Lady Lyndon. We would be delighted to attend."

Chapter Nine

That night, long after the rest of the house was quiet, Caroline sat alone in her bedroom window seat, looking out at the house next to theirs. The house she now knew was occupied by the Sewards.

By Lord Lyndon. Or Justin, as her stubborn, silly mind still insisted on thinking of him.

She sighed and pleated the velvet of her dressing gown between her restless fingers.

Harry Seward she was not so very worried about, despite the calf eyes he made at Phoebe all afternoon. He had generally been inebriated when he met her at the Golden Feather. Justin, though, was another case altogether. He had been all too sober. Certainly a first for any old friend of Lawrence's, if indeed that was what he was.

Why, oh why, did he have to come here to Wycombe? Why could he not have gone to Bath or Brighton, or any one of a dozen other watering places? They were more fashionable.

But no. He was here, right next door in the white mansion his brother had complained was too small.

It would be quite disastrous if he were to recognize her as Mrs. Archer, both for herself and for innocent Phoebe. He seemed like a kind man, but he *was* an earl, with a position in Society to uphold. He would never let his mother associate with a woman who had owned a gaming house, or her sister.

Caroline leaned her aching head against the cool glass of the window, still watching the darkened house across the garden. The most sensible thing would be to stay far away from Lord Lyndon and his family, so that he would have no opportunity for unfortunate recognitions. Yet how could she do that, when Lady Lyndon had invited them for a card party the very next evening?

No, she could not deprive Phoebe of this social opportunity. It had been all the girl could talk of during supper, how charming the Sewards were, how much she liked Sarah Bellweather, and how she looked forward to the party.

Caroline remembered Phoebe's shining eyes and knew she could never disappoint her so.

"He did not remember me this afternoon," she whispered. They sat next to each other in the tea shop for more than an hour, and he had not once shown any flash of recognition or suspicion. Of course, she had been wearing her large bonnet, and she had tried not to look at him too long or speak with him too much.

It might prove more difficult to be evasive if she was seated across from him at a card table, with no sheltering hat. But she had to try, for Phoebe's sake.

Perhaps for her own sake, as well.

She had liked Lord Lyndon in London, had been drawn to him in a way she never had been to a man in the past. Not even Lawrence.

She liked him even more here at the seaside. Not

only was he handsome; he was quite funny, in a wry way. If she had not been so intent on avoiding detection, she would have laughed aloud at many of his observations. He had a quiet, authoritative way with his brother that she wished she could emulate with Phoebe. He was solicitous of his mother, polite with the bevy of Bellweathers, even the obnoxious Lady Bellweather.

Yes, Caroline liked him very much indeed. If things had been different, if she were an ordinary, respectable widow, she would be looking forward to tomorrow night's gathering with great eagerness.

Truth to tell, she still looked forward to it, even if the eagerness was mixed with a healthy amount of dread.

Justin sat alone in the darkened library after everyone else was abed. It had been a rather exhausting struggle to persuade Harry to retire to his room rather than go out and send notes to Miss Lane, but Justin found he was not tired at all. His mind kept going over the rather puzzling afternoon at the tea shop.

The day began as expected. They went to meet the Bellweathers after luncheon for a stroll along the promenade, and he dutifully escorted Miss Sarah Bellweather. She was certainly a pretty girl, with a rather pert air about her, but Justin had not been able to summon up more than a polite interest in her. When she wasted no time in telling him she intended never to marry, he found that that suited him very well, and they thereafter engaged in perfectly polite conversation about the weather.

Then they met Mrs. Aldritch and her sister, the very vivid Miss Lane.

He had felt . . . *something* when he met Mrs. Aldritch. A jolt of attraction, almost of recognition. And he had thought she felt it, too. Her gloved hand had trembled when he bowed over it.

But she was quiet and stiff in the tea shop, especially after she learned he had known Larry. She answered all his attempts to draw her into conversation with soft murmurs. He hardly even got a look at her face; she was always turning away beneath her cursed bonnet. All he had been given were intriguing glimpses of dark eyes and moonlight-colored hair.

Perhaps she was simply shy. Quite unlike another woman of his recent acquaintance, a woman he had also found intriguing. There had been nothing shy about Mrs. Archer.

Justin laughed at the absurdity of it. In all his years in India, there had been only one woman he was remotely interested in, a widow who had soon deserted him for wedded bliss with an elderly colonel. Now, after only a few weeks back in England, he met not one but two lovely, intriguing women.

Perhaps it only meant that after four years of thinking about what he wanted, needed from his life, it was time to start living it.

And tomorrow evening, at the card party, he would have another chance to try to draw out Mrs. Aldritch.

Phoebe lay awake in her bed, tossing and turning, too excited to sleep. It had truly been a most eventful day, everything she had hoped for at dull old Mrs. Medlock's School. She had met what was surely the most handsome man in England. She giggled into her pillow when she recalled Harry Seward's brown curls and lovely hazel eyes.

He had excellent fashion sense, as well; she had never before seen anything so elegant as his orange brocade waistcoat.

He didn't seem to be much of a talker, but that hardly mattered. She had quite enough to say for both of them.

And she was to see him again tomorrow evening! At a card party in his own house. This holiday was turning out even finer than she had hoped it would.

Phoebe turned over onto her side, to look at the wall her room shared with Caroline's chamber. If only she could find someone for her sister, so that she could be just as happy as Phoebe was now. . . .

Of course! Phoebe sat straight up in her excitement. Mr. Seward's brother. Oh, why had she not thought of it sooner? It was so perfect.

Lord Lyndon seemed too serious by half, but Caro appeared to like that. He was very handsome for an older gentleman, *and* he had a title.

"Caroline, Countess of Lyndon," Phoebe whispered. Then she giggled again.

Oh, yes. This summer was just getting better and better.

Chapter Ten

"Isn't it exciting, Caro? Our first party here! I thought this day would last forever and the evening would never come."

Caroline smiled as she watched Phoebe bounce on her dressing table bench while Mary attempted to dress her hair. It had been a very long time since Caroline had eagerly anticipated any social gathering, but Phoebe's enthusiasm infected her. Her nervousness at seeing Lord Lyndon again, her apprehension that he might recognize her, was almost, but not quite, overcome by the pleasurable sense of expectation.

"Now, Phoebe," she warned, "you know that this is not exactly a grand ball. It is only supper and cards."

"That is more than there ever was at school!" Phoebe tried to turn her head to look at Caroline.

"Miss Phoebe, stop that!" Mary said sternly. "If you keep fidgeting about like that your hair will be all lopsided."

"I am sorry, Mary, dear," Phoebe answered, sounding not at all contrite. "I will sit very still now." She finally managed to cease bobbing and face the mirror again, allowing Mary to finish twisting her curls atop her head and fastening them with pearl-headed pins and white ribbons.

Caroline went back to sorting through her own jewel case. She wondered which would go best with her gown, her pearls or the amethyst pendant.

Then, beneath a gold and garnet brooch, she saw a flash of green fire. She reached down and took up the pair of emerald earrings. The earrings she had worn at the Golden Feather the night she met Lord Lyndon.

She held the stones on her palm, turning them a bit so they sparkled in the candlelight. Really, she should have sold them; they were so distinctive in design that she could hardly wear them again.

But she had not.

"Caro, they're beautiful!"

Startled, Caroline looked up to see Phoebe standing behind her. She was so distracted that she had not noticed her sister's coiffure had been completed.

"Can I wear them?" Phoebe continued. "They would go so well with my gown."

Caroline pushed the earrings back into the box and shut the lid firmly. "Certainly not! They are too old for you. You have Mama's locket, and it looks lovely."

Phoebe touched the gold oval hanging on the chain at her throat. "But those earrings would add such dash to my ensemble."

Caroline laughed and stood to hug her sister. "My dear, I am sure you will be the most dashing young lady there!" And indeed she would be. Or at the very least, the most distinctive. Caroline had persuaded her to wear one of her more subdued gowns, a sea-green muslin, but it was trimmed with such copious amounts of lace, so many white satin bows, that Phoebe was sure to be noticed.

"Are you quite certain?" she asked anxiously, fluffing some of the lace on her sleeve. "You do not think the color too . . . pale?"

"Not at all. It is very stylish." Caroline linked her arm in Phoebe's and hurried her toward the door, anxious to have her away before she could decide to change her clothes again. "Now, we must be going, my dear, or we shall be late and miss the supper."

She was not here yet.

Justin paused just out of sight before he entered the drawing room, surveying the guests assembled there. His mother and Lady Bellweather sat talking by the window. Sarah stood behind them, looking pretty in pink silk but rather bored. Harry paced restlessly by the empty fireplace, tugging and smoothing at his waistcoat, a black satin embroidered with copious yellow butterflies.

The rest of the guests, a few friends of his mother's and their sons and daughters, stood about in small groups, talking, laughing, waiting for supper to begin.

Mrs. Aldritch was not among them.

Justin felt a prick of disappointment. He had been looking forward to seeing her again, without the wide brim of her bonnet obscuring her face.

His gaze went to the clock on the fireplace mantel. It was almost time for supper, but not quite. Surely they would be here very soon.

His mother saw him then, and called out "Justin! There you are, dear. Lady Bellweather was just telling me of a concert to be held on Saturday evening that I think we should attend. It is a program of Renaissance songs, which I know you enjoy."

Justin smiled at her and came into the room to stand next to her. "Of course, Mother. It sounds delightful."

"Do you think perhaps Mrs. Aldritch and her sister might enjoy it, as well? I did hear Mrs. Aldritch say that she was very fond of music."

Lady Bellweather gave a loud, disapproving sniff.

Before Justin could answer, the two ladies in question appeared in the doorway, as if summoned by the mention of their names. Mrs. Aldritch was turned away slightly to hand her shawl to a footman, while Miss Lane bounced merrily on her feet, her gaze lightly skimming over the crowd.

Then Mrs. Aldritch faced the room, and he saw that she was even prettier than she had been in the tea shop. Her hair was caught up in soft, pale waves by a bandeau of ribbon and seed pearls. Her gown, a subdued cinnamon-brown silk, was perfectly respectable, but showed off a white throat and sloping shoulders.

A small, polite smile curved her rose-pink lips as she looked around, one kid-gloved hand reaching out to catch her sister's arm and still that bouncing.

Amelia stood and started forward eagerly, tugging an unresisting Justin along in her wake.

But they were not quite fast enough to be the first to reach them. Harry beat them handily, rushing up in a blur of black and yellow to bow politely over Mrs. Aldritch's hand and eagerly over Miss Lane's.

"I do say!" he said breathlessly. "So good to see you, both of you, again. I must say I never . . ."

Justin nudged Harry a bit to get him to cease prattling and release Miss Lane's hand.

"Good evening, Lady Lyndon, Lord Lyndon, Mr. Seward," Mrs. Aldritch said softly. "It was indeed very good of you to invite us, but I fear we are rather late. I do apologize."

"Not at all," Amelia said. "We were only just now thinking of going in to supper, my dear. Justin, would you escort Mrs. Aldritch? And Harry, I do believe you are to escort Miss Bellweather."

Harry blushed a bright, unflattering pink, and frowned. "Miss Bellweather! Dash it all, Mother, I did say . . ."

"Yes," his mother said firmly. "Miss Bellweather, who is waiting for you now. Miss Lane, do allow me to introduce you to your dinner partner, Mr. Allen."

Amelia led Miss Lane away, while Harry shuffled off reluctantly to Miss Bellweather, who looked just as crestfallen to have him for a supper partner as he was to *not* have Miss Lane. This left Justin quite alone with Mrs. Aldritch.

Her dark eyes seemed rather anxious as she watched her sister walk away. Justin tried to smile at her reassuringly.

"I do apologize for my brother's puppyish behavior," he said. "I will speak to him and tell him to cease bothering your sister at once."

She laughed wryly. "I must confess, I fear your brother's . . . botherations are not entirely unwelcomed by my sister. I have spoken to her, but she is still quite young and rather headstrong."

Young and headstrong. Words that described Harry perfectly.

Words that once would have described Justin, as well.

He looked across the room to where Harry stood dutifully next to Miss Bellweather. Harry's gaze was avidly fastened onto Miss Lane, where she stood laughing and talking with Mr. Allen. Every impatience, every passionate emotion was clearly written across his face.

Lud, had he, Justin, ever really been *that* young?

"So you knew my husband, Lord Lyndon?" Mrs. Aldritch said, drawing his attention back to her. She watched him closely, seriously. Her face was as blank and cool as Harry's was open and obvious.

"Larry Aldritch. Yes, I knew him. We were all friends, he and I, and Freddie Reed and James Burne-Jones. Back before I went out to India." He shook his head. "That seems a hundred years ago now."

"Yes. A hundred years at least."

Justin looked down at her. She was so still, so dignified. How had she ever ended up married to such a wild youth as Larry Aldritch? Surely this woman, who seemed such a lady from the top of her pale hair to the hem of her brown silk skirt, had experienced much difficulty tolerating the sort of behavior Larry had gotten up to.

Of course! That must be the reason she seemed so cool to him, so tense in his presence. She remembered him as being a friend of Larry's, and disapproved.

Perhaps that was the explanation for the very odd sense of recognition he felt around her, as well. Maybe he had met her back then and had been too foxed to recall the meeting clearly.

Could he have insulted her in some way?

By Jove, but he hoped not.

"Did we meet before?" he said slowly, half dreading her answer.

She shook her head. "No, Lord Lyndon, not that I recall. I did meet some of my husband's friends, of course, but I seldom went out. I do not remember you, though I do remember Mr. Reed and Mr. Burne-Jones. You will have to tell me of your . . . adventures together sometime."

"So Larry never spoke of me?" he persisted. He had a burning desire to know what he might have done to insult her, so he could make it right.

"No. But then, it was a long time ago. I have long forgotten most of my husband's ramblings." Her delicate jaw tightened.

Justin's stomach unknotted in relief. She *hadn't* seen him at his very worst, then. He forced himself to give a light laugh. "Well, Mrs. Aldritch, I fear you would be quite bored by my tales of adventures, as you call them. They were all very commonplace and dull."

"As the follies of youth so often are," she answered, smiling at him for the first time that evening. "I know that very well. But I am sure that your *true* adventures in India were hardly commonplace at all."

Justin shook his head, remembering the mosquitoes, the heat, and the appalling rain of the monsoons. "Some of them were very dull indeed, I assure you."

"At the tea shop yesterday your mother said you hunted tigers and fought battles with rebelling natives, where you saved a colonel's life and won copious medals. That you survived fevers and plagues. That hardly seems dull to me."

"First of all, they were hardly battles. More like skirmishes," he protested. "And I spent four years in India, Mrs. Aldritch. Of those, perhaps only six months were exciting."

"Exciting or dull, I should like to hear about them nonetheless."

He looked at her, surprised and rather pleased. "Would you really?"

"Of course. I have never left England, and I probably never shall. I would love to hear of other lands. Other lives."

The butler appeared to announce that supper was served.

Justin held out his arm to Mrs. Aldritch, and she slipped her hand softly into the crook of his elbow, allowing him to escort her into the dining room.

"I would be happy to tell you of India," he said, as he seated her at her place at the table. "Sometime soon?"

She seemed to hesitate for a second, then slowly nodded her head. "Soon, Lord Lyndon."

Chapter Eleven

"Has your mother known Lady Lyndon very long?" Phoebe asked Sarah Bellweather. The two of them sat in one of the cushioned window seats after supper, watching the others play cards and whispering together.

"Forever, it seems." Sarah sighed. "They were quite the bosom bows when I came home from school. They expected me to marry Lord Lyndon, you know."

"No!" Phoebe, shocked, looked over to where Lord Lyndon played whist with her sister, Lady Lyndon, and Mr. Allen. He said something to Caroline, who nodded and smiled.

How could he possibly marry Sarah Bellweather when Phoebe had picked him out especially for her own sister!

"But . . . he's so old," she said faintly.

Sarah grimaced. "I know. And I intend never to marry. I want to be an archaeologist."

Phoebe found this even more shocking than the thought of Sarah marrying old Lord Lyndon. Even though she had been widely considered the most daring girl at Mrs. Medlock's School, Phoebe had never thought of doing anything but marrying.

Her esteem for Sarah Bellweather grew by the moment.

"You mean you want to dig about in the dirt for old bones?" she asked, having only the vaguest idea about what archaeologists did.

"Yes, and old treasure, too. I have been reading all about ancient civilizations, and I have corresponded with several members of the Antiquarian Society in London. It is my greatest dream," Sarah said wistfully. "But I fear it will never come true. Mama thinks all a lady should think about are babies and needlework. She's been going on for weeks about how I should be charming to Lord Lyndon."

"You . . . you're not really going to marry him, are you?" Phoebe asked, her gaze still on Caroline and Lord Lyndon. Caroline laughed, actually *laughed,* at something he was saying to her. "You absolutely cannot!"

"I know that. I even told him I intend never to marry, just in case his mother had the same idea as mine. He was really very nice about it, and he agreed that we probably would not suit."

Phoebe smiled in relief. That was all right, then. Lyndon was safe for Caroline.

"Now, though, I fear Mama has set her sights on Harry Seward for me," Sarah continued. "She keeps saying that the brother of an earl is better than no connection to an earl at all."

What! Phoebe almost leaped out of her seat. No, that could not be! Harry Seward was hers; he admired *her.*

Didn't he?

She turned to look at Harry where he sat playing cassino. She had little experience with gentlemen, it was true, but surely she could not have imagined his admiring glances?

"And what do you think of the idea of marrying Mr. Seward?" she asked.

Sarah gave an unladylike little snort. "That is even more absurd than the idea of marrying Lord Lyndon! Why, Harry Seward would not know a first-century amphora if it hit him over the head. No, I just need to disabuse Mama of all her ridiculous notions of marrying me off."

"I see. Yes." Phoebe sat back against the wall, tapping her finger thoughtfully against her chin.

"Oh, my dears, I win this trick!" Amelia cried delightedly, laying down her cards. "That means Mr. Allen and I have beat you most handily, Justin."

Justin laughed. "So you have, Mother! I fear I let Mrs. Aldritch down, after working so hard to persuade her to partner me." He looked sheepishly at Mrs. Aldritch, who smiled as she laid down her own cards.

"It was my own fault entirely, Lord Lyndon," she answered. "I have not played whist for so long, my skills have become quite rusty."

"No, it is Mother's fault for being such a card-sharper," Justin teased.

"Lord Lyndon!" Lady Bellweather cried from the next table. "You should not say such things about your own mother. A cardsharper, indeed!"

"Nonsense, Dolly," Lady Lyndon said, looking rather pleased at the thought of being a "sharper." "I *am* quite a dab hand at whist. Now, my dears, I find myself in need of some refreshment."

"Shall I fetch you some tea, Mother?" Justin said, folding his cards neatly and rising to his feet.

"So good of you, dear! Perhaps you would escort Mrs. Aldritch to the refreshment table, too? I am sure she must be fatigued after sitting for so long."

Justin peered closely at his mother, but she looked back at him steadily, all innocence. Could she possibly have suddenly switched her matchmaking machinations from Miss Bellweather to Mrs. Aldritch?

Of course she could. And Justin found that he did not half mind the idea of being thrown together with Mrs. Aldritch. In fact, he rather liked it.

"*Would* you care to accompany me, Mrs. Aldritch?" he asked her.

"Thank you, Lord Lyndon. I think I would like some tea." As she took his arm and they set off across the room to where the refreshments were laid out, she leaned closer and said quietly, "I would also like to find my sister. I fear I played too intently at the game, and she and Miss Bellweather have quite disappeared."

He looked around the room quickly and saw that she was right. Miss Lane and Miss Bellweather were gone.

And so was Harry. He no longer played at the cassino table where Justin had left him after supper.

"I am afraid my brother is also missing," he muttered.

"Oh, no! You don't think they all would have gone off to get into some mischief, do you?" The fine, fair skin of her forehead wrinkled in a concerned frown.

"With Harry, anything is possible," Justin answered ruefully.

"As with Phoebe. Oh, I am a terrible chaperon! I should have known better."

"Not at all, Mrs. Aldritch. I am certain they have just gone into the library or some such place."

"Phoebe? In a library?"

Somehow, Justin could not picture Harry there, either. "Perhaps not the library. But there are a great many other rooms in this house. I could search for them, if it would make you feel more at ease."

She nodded decisively. "I will go with you, Lord Lyndon. I do not have a good feeling about this at all."

"Mr. Seward! Do be careful. Those rocks look slippery," Phoebe cried, clasping her hands together tightly as she watched Harry climb out on some rocky outcroppings over a small, sheltered cove.

He had claimed there was smugglers' treasure hidden there, just beneath the rocks, when he had come to sit with her and Sarah after his card game ended. When he offered to show it to them, it seemed a fine lark.

Now Phoebe was not so sure. Harry's thin-soled evening shoes slipped and slid on the wet rocks as he inched his way out.

"Oh, do be careful!" she called again.

Sarah Bellweather was more blunt. "You're a silly fool, Harry Seward," she said, pausing in drawing a stick through the sand to watch his hapless progress. "There's probably no treasure there at all."

"There is!" Harry shouted back. "I saw it just last night. Silks, no doubt, and brandy and wine."

"Well, even if there is a treasure, I'm sure the smugglers would not take kindly to your stealing it," Sarah said matter-of-factly. "They would probably shoot you down."

"Shoot him!" Phoebe cried, appalled. "Oh, Mr. Seward, do come back, please."

"Smugglers don't frighten me, Miss Lane," Harry answered stoutly, kneeling down and stretching his hand between an outcropping of two rocks. "I think I just about have something now. Yes, I definitely feel something—" He broke off with a high-pitched scream. "Ahhh!" he shrieked, falling down flat on his face, his hand still caught in the rocks.

"Whatever are you carrying on about?" Sarah called, her eyes wide.

"It bit off my hand!" Harry screamed in reply, flailing his black satin-clad legs about.

Phoebe felt herself tilting swiftly into hysterics. The man she was falling in love with was dying right before her eyes!

It was just like *The Sins of Lady Lydia*.

She turned and fled up the incline toward the Sewards' house, tears streaming down her face. All she could think of was finding Caroline and making her save the day, while Harry flailed and screamed and Sarah called out futile instructions to him to keep breathing.

"They are not in here." Caroline pushed aside the last large plant in the conservatory and fell down wearily onto a wrought-iron chaise. "I feel we have searched everywhere."

"We have, almost." Justin brushed some flower petals from his hair and sat down in a chair next to her. "They were not in the library or the morning room or the upstairs gallery. The servants have not seen them. The only place we have not searched is the attic, and I am sure Harry would not muss his attire by going up there."

"We did not look in the garden."

"You can see almost the entire garden from here."

Indeed she could. One wall of the conservatory was made of windows, and through them was the whole vista of the garden, sloping down to the sea along a gentle incline.

Caroline leaned back to survey the scene laid out before her so perfectly. It was a magical night, with the moon shining down on the manicured gardens and the wild sea beyond. The water shimmered in the silver-capped darkness.

It would be so easy to sit here in silence with Lord Lyndon—Justin—watching the scene of perfect beauty as it shifted and changed all through the night. It had been a delightful evening, and he had lulled her into a dangerous comfort with his presence.

Dangerous because if she lost her wariness, her ever-present knowledge of the secrets she had to keep, she would be so vulnerable to the spell he wove.

The spell he was weaving about her so seductively right now, just by sitting quietly beside her. She was acutely aware of his warmth, of the spicy scent of his soap.

A warm lassitude stole over her, wrought by the

beautiful night, the wonderful normality of the party—and the man beside her. She wanted to turn to him, to put her arms about him and draw his lips down to hers. If she could only feel his kiss, the safety of his arms about her, holding her close. . . .

What was she thinking of!

Caroline sat straight up, trying to shake off the sweet, seductive thoughts that wound around her. Her sister was missing, probably off getting into some mischief, and all she was doing was sitting here, dreaming of kissing the man who could expose her past and cause them ruin.

She stood up quickly, obviously startling Lord Lyndon, who looked as moonstruck as she felt.

"Per-perhaps we should search the garden anyway," she said swiftly.

He rose to his feet, as well, standing next to her. "Of course, if you like, Mrs. Aldritch. I am sure they must be someplace close by."

"I do not know what else to do. What if they—" She was interrupted by the faint but unmistakable sound of a scream coming from outside the conservatory.

It sounded to Caroline's panicked ears like Phoebe. She looked about frantically for a door, but Justin was there before her, throwing open the glass door and hurrying out into the night.

Caroline followed and saw Phoebe running up the slope from the seashore, her pale green gown a flash of light against the darkness.

"Phoebe!" she cried, running toward her sister.

Tears streamed down Phoebe's face, and her hair fell disheveled from its pins and ribbons. One lace ruffle was torn on her sleeve.

Caroline's first, fierce thought was that Harry Seward had somehow hurt her sister, and she was going to have to kill him for it.

Phoebe reached her and threw herself, sobbing, into Caroline's arms.

"Caro!" she wept, her cheek wet where she pressed it against the silk of Caroline's dress. "You have to fix it!"

"Fix what, darling? What has happened?" She looked at Justin over Phoebe's bent head and saw that his face was tight and angry in the moonlight.

Obviously, he was thinking the same thing that she was, and he was utterly furious. Perhaps she would not have to kill Harry after all; his brother would do it for her, most handily.

Caroline shook Phoebe lightly by the shoulders. "Phoebe! Stop this now, and tell me what has happened."

Phoebe shook her head wildly, sending the rest of her curls tumbling free over her shoulders. "He is *dead*!"

Chapter Twelve

"Tell me, Harry. Is your brain still in your head, or did you somehow leave it behind in London?"

Harry, seated across the library desk from Justin, slouched down deeper into his chair and pouted. "Really Justin, I don't know what you're saying."

Justin, completely exasperated, planted his hands firmly on the desk with a loud slap. "I am saying that anyone with a brain, with *half* a brain for that matter, would never have taken two young ladies down to the shore in the middle of the night. Anything could have happened! One of you might have been killed or seriously injured."

Harry held up his bandaged hand. "I *was* injured! And I am in far too much pain for your hectoring."

"Pain! You merely got your hand caught between two rocks, where you had no business putting it in the first place. Then you had such hysterics that you almost frightened poor Miss Lane to death."

"I certainly never meant to frighten her at all," Harry said sheepishly. "I would never hurt such a sweet angel. I merely wanted to show her and Miss Bellweather the, er, smugglers' treasure."

"That part makes it even worse. If that 'treasure' did indeed belong to smugglers', they would have shot you on sight. And God knows what they would have done to the ladies."

Harry's gaze slid away. "Actually, Justin . . ."

Justin sighed. "What now?"

"There never was a treasure of any sort there. There wasn't anything there but seaweed."

"You mean to say you took those girls out there just to show off?"

"I would not put it exactly that way."

"I would. You have hardly been living in a wilderness all your life, Harry. You know how deeply improper your actions were, not to mention dangerous."

"It won't happen again!"

"You are damn right it won't. I intend to watch you very closely from now on, Harry. And if I so much as see you dancing with Miss Lane without her sister's permission, I will send you off to India."

"Now, really, Justin! You can't treat me like I'm in leading strings. I am an adult."

"Show me you can behave like one, then, and I will treat you as one."

"Justin—"

Justin held up his hand in a sharp gesture, stopping the flow of protests. "I don't have time for this now. I have a call to make."

"What sort of a call?"

"Not that it is any of your business, young Harry, but I am going to call on Mrs. Aldritch."

Harry's demeanor cautiously lit up. He slid to the edge of his seat. "Mrs. Aldritch? Perhaps if I could go with you and apologize in person . . ."

"I do not think so. Mrs. Aldritch was very upset

when she found her sister missing, and I doubt she would want to see you today."

Harry looked crestfallen. "Oh."

Justin's anger faded, and he relented just a bit. "Perhaps tomorrow Mrs. Aldritch and Miss Lane would agree to go with us on our picnic with Mother and the Bellweathers."

"Oh!" Harry cried. "Do you really think so?"

"I will ask her."

"I never meant any harm, Caro. I promise!" Phoebe sat next to her sister on the settee, her hands pressed to her tearstained cheeks. "I would not have worried you for all the world."

Caroline sighed. "I know you *meant* no harm, darling. But did they not teach you of the proprieties at Mrs. Medlock's? Of common sense, for heaven's sake! You must know better than to go down to the shore in the middle of the night. Why, there could have been any sort of criminals about! Not to mention what could have happened to your reputation."

"I know, I know! It was silly of me, I know, but when Mr. Seward said something about a treasure, I simply had to see it. It was just like *Secrets of a Windswept Sea.*"

Caroline knew then that she was going to have to go through Phoebe's chamber and dispose of every horrid novel. She pressed a handkerchief into Phoebe's trembling hand, and said, "You must never leave a party, or anyplace else, without telling me first. I was very worried."

"But I was not *alone* with Mr. Seward, Caro! Miss Bellweather was with us." At Caroline's stern glance, Phoebe subsided again, and said meekly, "I promise I will not do it again."

"I do hope not. You know that Wycombe is a very small place, darling. It would never do to have people think you are, well, less than proper. A young lady's reputation is so very important, you know."

Phoebe wiped at her eyes and nodded. "I know you are depending on me, Caro, and I will not fail you. I would never do anything to demean our family."

"I know you would not. Just, please, be very careful in the future. Especially where Mr. Seward is concerned." Caroline leaned over to kiss Phoebe's cheek, then gave her a reassuring pat on the hand. "Now, why don't you go upstairs and wash your face? Perhaps we could go out for ices this afternoon."

Phoebe smiled. "I would like that," she said, and left the room quickly, obviously relieved that the scolding was over.

When she was gone, Caroline tucked her left foot beneath her right knee on the settee and rubbed at the scar on her ankle wearily. How very complicated chaperonage was! Not at all as simple and enjoyable as she had thought it was going to be. Never could she have imagined a scene such as the one she faced last night.

She closed her eyes as she recalled rushing down to the shore with Lord Lyndon and the hysterical Phoebe. The sight of Mr. Seward flailing about with his hand caught between some rocks, shrieking fit to raise the dead, had been so very comical she had had to fight to keep from laughing aloud.

Worse, she had seen the same sort of repressed laughter on Lord Lyndon's face as he worked to free his brother's hand.

She *did* laugh now, alone in her drawing room, at the memory of that absurd tableau.

But she knew very well that it would not have been in the least comical if the entire company had witnessed the scene. No, it would have been very embarrassing, and it would surely have given rise to gossip.

Thank the stars for Sarah Bellweather. She was certainly a cool and calculating thinker, unlike her silly mother. She had concocted a plan for Lyndon to slip his brother up the back stairs and get him tidied up before taking him back to the party, and for Caroline and Phoebe to go back home through the garden. She then told the guests that Phoebe had a terrible headache, and her sister was now taking her home after she had spent an hour in the retiring room with Sarah. Crisis neatly averted.

Phoebe was lucky to have a friend like Sarah, if she was going to insist on being so featherheaded.

But would the next disaster be so easy to avoid?

Caroline rubbed her hand on her ankle. Running the Golden Feather had never been as complicated as this.

Mary came into the room, interrupting Caroline's whirling thoughts.

"There's a caller, madam," she said, waving the silver tray that held one card.

A caller was the last thing Caroline wanted to deal with just then. She had far too many things to worry about as it was without having to make polite conversation over tea.

She supposed she had to be civil, though, if she wanted to be accepted into the center of Wycombe's little society.

"Who is it, Mary?" she asked, swinging her foot back to the floor and smoothing her skirt over her legs.

"It's that Lord Lyndon," Mary sniffed. "The one that came to call in London."

"Mary!" Caroline cried, horrified. "You aren't supposed to even mention London. What if he heard you?"

"He could hardly hear me, madam. He's out on the doorstep."

"You left Lord Lyndon out on the doorstep!"

"Well, where else was I to put him? There's no foyer to speak of in this little place."

"Show him in, Mary, at once. And have some tea sent in, as well."

"Very good, madam."

Mary left in a huff, and soon reappeared with Lord Lyndon behind her. He seemed none the worse for having been left standing on the doorstep. "Lord Lyndon, madam," Mary announced, then promptly ran off again.

Caroline smiled at him, hoping that her hair was not mussed. She had scarce had time to even look in a mirror all day. "Good afternoon, Lord Lyndon. Won't you please be seated?"

"Thank you, Mrs. Aldritch." He sat down in a chair placed directly in a beam of sunlight, and Caroline saw that his face looked rather pale and drawn, as if he had not slept much last night.

He looked as weary as she felt.

"I have come to apologize for my brother's behavior," he said.

"Apologize? Oh, Lord Lyndon, it is hardly your

fault that your brother did something . . . less than advisable."

"I feel that it was. I knew that Harry's behavior of late has been quite unpredictable, and I failed to keep a strict eye on him last night. As a result, your evening was ruined, and things could have ended much worse."

"The evening was hardly *ruined*," she protested. "I had a delightful time at your mother's party. And if you are to blame for not watching your brother, then I am also to blame for failing to watch Phoebe." Caroline realized then that what she was saying was true. After a long night of self-recrimination, she saw that she could not possibly be responsible for every action of Phoebe's. Any more than her parents could have been responsible for Caroline, once upon a time. "We are not their nursemaids."

"That is true." He nodded slowly, obviously still not completely convinced. "I would still like to say I am sorry, though, and promise you that it will not happen again. I gave Harry a scolding this morning. One that I hope he will not soon forget."

"Apology accepted, then, if it will make you feel better. And I also gave Phoebe a few things to think about. I am just glad that the smugglers did not appear last night! Now that would have ruined the party in truth."

Lord Lyndon laughed. "As to that, I can assure you that there was never any danger of smugglers showing up."

"Really?"

"Really. Harry told me he made up the entire corker about smugglers' treasure just to impress the young ladies."

Caroline stared at him, feeling laughter of her own bubbling up. "He . . . made it all up?"

"I fear so."

"The rascal!" She did laugh then; she could not seem to help it. The whole thing was so richly absurd. "Phoebe would be so angry if she knew. She truly feared for Mr. Seward's life."

"Oh, his life was never in any danger, though he certainly carried on as if it were. I hope this entire situation has taught him a lesson."

"I am sure it has." Caroline wiped at her laughter-damp eyes.

"And now I can come to the second, and much more pleasant, reason for this visit."

She looked up at him curiously. "A second reason, Lord Lyndon?"

"Yes. Mother wanted to see the Roman ruins outside of town and is organizing a picnic there tomorrow. The Bellweathers are coming, and Mother and I thought you might care to accompany us as well."

Hmm. Another invitation. Caroline felt a warm, satisfied, nervous feeling blossom deep inside of her. What could it all mean? Was it simply Lady Lyndon being kind to the daughters of her old friend? Or could it possibly be something more? Could the invitation be Lord Lyndon's idea? Could he . . . admire her?"

She forced down a silly giggle, and studied him closely, searching for any signs of admiration at all.

Sadly, he merely looked polite.

"I have heard the ruins are quite picturesque," she said.

"Indeed. I believe they are an ancient bathhouse and villa, or at least parts of them."

"I take it Mr. Seward will be along, as well."

"If he is not sulking in his room, yes. But you need have no fear that he will lure your sister away, Mrs. Aldritch. I promise you that I will tie him to the picnic hamper if I have to."

"Then you do not think he will suddenly discover ancient *Roman* smugglers' treasure?" she teased.

Lord Lyndon gave a startled laugh at her little joke. "Let us hope not."

"Then I should like to go, and I am sure Phoebe will as well."

"We shall call for you tomorrow morning at ten, then, if that would be convenient."

"I will look forward to it."

Oh, yes, I certainly will, her mind whispered.

Chapter Thirteen

Mrs. Aldritch looked most lovely in the afternoon sun. Like a portrait of a fairy queen examining her forest domain.

Justin shook his head ruefully at his fantastical thoughts. He had never been at all prone to being poetical, had always scorned men who went about spouting verses about ladies' eyelashes and such.

But he had to admit that if he *were* to start composing rhymes, Mrs. Aldritch would be a most delightful inspiration.

She sat on a large, flat rock overlooking the villa ruins, watching her sister and Miss Bellweather scurry about, examining the mosaic floor. She held a white, lacy parasol over her head, and the sun filtered through the patterns of the lace, casting shifting shadows on her face and the skirt of her sky-blue gown.

The short waves of her pale hair, though bound back neatly with a wide blue ribbon, shifted and shimmered in the breeze.

But her expression was far too serious for such a beautiful day, such a fetching pose. She was frowning a bit, her gaze far away even as she looked at the girls. She looked as if she did not see the pretty scene before her at all, but something invisible to everyone else.

Something worrisome.

He had the strongest urge to go to her, to take her hand and make her tell him what it was that worried her. He wanted to erase that frown and hear her laugh again, as she had when he told her of Harry's fib. She had a wonderful laugh, warm and rich, though seemingly a bit rusty from misuse.

It appeared that whatever her life had been since Larry Aldritch died, it had not involved much laughter. She usually looked much as she did now, worried and distant.

Justin found it brought out the latent white knight in him. The one with the irresistible urge to make unhappy fair damsels smile.

She looked up and saw him watching her. A smile *did* appear on her lips, albeit a small one, and her brow smoothed.

"Lord Lyndon," she called, "is it not a fine day?"

"Lovely," he answered, coming forward to sit down on the grass at her feet. He stretched out his legs along the ground, enjoying the warmth of the sun.

"I cannot thank you enough for inviting us today. Phoebe looks much better in the fresh air. I feared she would never quit crying yesterday."

"And Harry looks much chastened." Justin gestured toward where Harry sat with his mother, Lady Bellweather, and the two younger Bellweather girls. Harry was apparently meant to be minding the girls while the ladies gossiped, and he held a large wax doll on his knee while one of the girls gave it tea from a tiny cup.

"Well, playing with dolls will do that to a man,

I suppose," she said wryly, whirling her parasol about by its carved handle.

"It is good for him. And those girls are absolute tartars; if anyone can keep him out of trouble, they can."

"Let us hope so." She turned her gaze back to her sister, the frown returning. "Phoebe is so very . . . lively. I do not want to curb her spirit, but I fear what trouble she may run into."

Justin nodded in deepest understanding. He felt exactly the same about Harry.

He glanced over at his brother and saw that Harry was watching Miss Lane again, his face full of longing. Justin knew that Harry fancied himself quite in love with her already, and certainly Justin was tempted to hand Harry and all his problems over to the care of a wife.

The only problem was that Miss Lane appeared to be every bit as prone to flights of fancy as Harry was. With her as a sister-in-law, Justin would not be solving his troubles; he would just be doubling them.

It was the very devil being the responsible one.

Mrs. Aldritch looked at him, her expression startled, and Justin realized with chagrin that he had spoken aloud.

He opened his mouth to apologize, but she forestalled him by saying, "It *is* the very devil, isn't it?"

Justin nodded. "When I was younger, I never dreamed I would be in this situation. Father and Edward, my older brother, took care of everything. Edward was just like Father—always steady and reliable, always getting me out of scrapes. Then they died."

"And you found yourself as the earl."

"Yes. With Harry to contend with. I know Mother wants me to solve everything for her, as Father did—be the 'head of the family.' But I lived alone for so long in India. I am not used to worrying about other people."

He looked down at the grass, suddenly ashamed at his outpouring of words to a near stranger. It was not seemly for an earl to appear unsure, and Mrs. Aldritch must be bored to hear him ramble on of his troubles.

But she didn't look bored. Her dark eyes watched him sympathetically, and she leaned toward him as if to hear all his words. He felt so very *comfortable* with her, felt he could tell her anything, and she would not judge as other people would. He felt as if he knew her.

She nodded. "Phoebe and I also lived apart for a long time. She was at school after our parents died, and I was with Lawrence, and then . . . then with relatives. I fear I concocted a perfect sister in my mind, one who was dutiful and obedient and always cheerful." She laughed humorlessly, mocking herself. "Things have not turned out the way I planned! Phoebe has her own way of doing things."

"That could describe Harry perfectly. His own way of doing things." Justin watched as Harry walked over to where Miss Lane and Miss Bellweather were still exploring the villa, the two little Bellweather girls tripping along behind him. He said something to Phoebe, who nodded, shook her head, then laughed. "My brother obviously admires your sister."

"Yes. But Phoebe is too young yet to be married."

"So is Harry. I wonder if a time in India might not be good for him, as it was for me."

"India?" Mrs. Aldritch tilted her head, looking on as Phoebe hauled one of the children up into her arms and twirled her about, the two of them giggling merrily. "You mustn't say anything about India in front of Phoebe. She would get visions of ivory palaces and rubies as big as hens' eggs into her head, and she would marry Mr. Seward just to go see them."

"At least if they were in India we wouldn't *know* what they were up to," Justin suggested. "Out of sight, out of mind?"

Mrs. Aldritch laughed, the worry fleeing from her face like the clouds from the sun.

Phoebe turned to look at them at the sound of that laughter, and waved. "Caro!" she called. "Do come and see these mosaics Miss Bellweather has been showing us. Those Romans were ever so naughty. Why didn't they teach us this at Mrs. Medlock's?"

Mrs. Aldritch waved back, then looked at Justin, one golden brow arched inquiringly. "Shall we join them, then, Lord Lyndon?"

"Of course." He leaped to his feet and held out his hand to help her rise from the rock. "I confess myself quite fascinated by, er, naughty Romans."

The "naughty" Roman mosaics were indeed fascinating, and quite extensive. Before Caroline realized it, they had left the others behind and found themselves in a quiet glade of trees. The green branches arched over the ruined tile floor, enclosing it in a thick silence.

Only the muted murmur of distant voices, the whisper of the wind through the leaves, and the click of their shoe heels on the tile reminded her that she was still in the real, human world. She felt as if she had fallen into some enchanted realm.

She lowered her parasol and stepped carefully over the cracked mosaic, acutely conscious of Justin close behind her. After their conversation, she felt strangely intimate toward him, bound in silken cords of understanding. She knew she could grow to understand him very well indeed, and he her.

That was a dangerous feeling. She could not afford to let him, or anyone else, truly know her. Truly know what her life had been about. It was a very lonely feeling.

Caroline stabbed at one of the tiles with the tip of her parasol. Well, she had been lonely for many years now; nothing would be different. She would just go on as before.

Justin knelt down beside her to examine part of the mosaic, interrupting her increasingly maudlin thoughts. "I cannot be sure, of course," he said, "but I do believe this scene is not quite as naughty as the others."

Caroline leaned over, pushing some of the tiles into place. "I believe you are right. It looks like a supper scene. See these grapes here. The colors are so vivid! As lovely as if they had been made yesterday."

"Lovely," he murmured. He was so close, his breath whispered coolly across her cheek.

Caroline pulled back, startled. She had not realized she had leaned so near to him.

She looked at him warily, to find that he watched her with equally startled eyes.

"Where did you come from, Mrs. Aldritch?" he whispered.

Oh, dear Lord, he knew. He recognized her; he knew the truth. It could be the only explanation for his astounded look. She fell back a step, away from him.

"C-come from?" she said. "Whatever do you mean?"

He shook his head in a bemused way, as if to clear it. "I am sorry. It must be this place, it seems so . . . otherworldly. You just don't seem quite like everyone else. Not quite human."

Caroline was confused. What did otherworldly glades have to do with gaming hells? "Not . . . human?" she said.

He laughed self-mockingly. "Now I have insulted you. Please believe me, Mrs. Aldritch, that is the last thing I would want to do. It is just that earlier I fancied you looked like a fairy queen, examining her domain. You seem to belong here, with the trees and the sky."

Caroline's tense shoulders slowly relaxed. Did this mean that he did *not* recognize her? She sat down on a crumbling old marble bench. "My mother used to say I was her changeling child. No one else in our family has such pale hair and such dark eyes."

"Perhaps that is it." He sat down next to her on the bench. "You must forgive me, Mrs. Aldritch. I promise you I am not generally prone to such flights of fancy, and I never speak to people I have just met in such a way. I think I must still have some of India in my blood. There *everything* seemed otherworldly, fraught with spirits."

"What is there to forgive?" Caroline answered,

with a small laugh. "Most people see me as a dull old matron now, as Phoebe's chaperon. I would much rather be a fairy queen."

"And that you are," he said, still looking at her with that bemused expression on his face. "That you are."

He looked as if he wanted to say something more, but a burst of chattering voices interrupted them. Phoebe, Sarah, Harry, and the two little girls came hurrying en masse into the glade.

"There you are, Caro!" Phoebe cried. "We feared you had fallen through these old floors or something. Lady Lyndon says we must hurry if we want our sweets."

"Yes," said Sarah, "or my mother will surely eat them *all*."

Caroline gave Justin one last smile, then went to take Phoebe's arm and go with her out of the glade. "Of course, darling. We were just enjoying the cool shade here."

"Oh, my dears," Lady Lyndon sighed, leaning back under the shade of the trees. "I cannot remember when I last had such a splendid afternoon."

Caroline had to agree with her. The afternoon had indeed been splendid. New friends, good food, sunshine—and Lord Lyndon.

She looked over to where he sat with Harry, Phoebe, and Sarah Bellweather, playing a game of Beggar My Neighbor with them. The afternoon breeze kept lifting the cards from the blanket, and he caught at them, laughing. A lock of sun-burnished hair fell across his forehead, and as he reached up to brush it back he caught her watching him.

He smiled at her, and his face, weather lined as it was from the Indian sun, looked endearingly boyish.

She could not help but smile back.

Then he turned away from her, back to the game.

"Would you tell me more about your mother, Mrs. Aldritch?" Lady Lyndon said, reaching for the last of the berry tarts. "After she married your father and I married Lord Lyndon, I fear we rather lost touch. I did receive a letter announcing your birth, and I sent one when each of my boys were born, but that was all."

"Mother was not much of a letter writer," Caroline answered. "We lived so quietly in the country that she feared to bore all her friends with her news."

"Now, that could never have been! Dear Margery was never dull. Your sister rather reminds me of her." They watched as Phoebe won the last of Harry's cards and crowed over her victory.

"Phoebe does look a great deal like Mother," Caroline answered uncertainly. She remembered her mother as being always quiet and proper, not vivid and crackling with energy as Phoebe was.

"As do you, Mrs. Aldritch," said Lady Lyndon. "When I heard of your birth, I must say I harbored a little dream that one day, when you were older, you would come to see me in London. I never had a daughter, you know, and I did so long for one. And you would meet Edward, my eldest, and then . . ." Her voice faded away, and she gave Caroline an embarrassed little smile. "But that was silly of me. I am very glad we have met *now*. Very glad indeed."

Caroline was surprised, and very touched, by her words. "I am glad we have met, too, Lady Lyndon."

"Then, my dear, perhaps you would like to accompany us to a concert on Saturday evening? It is a program of Renaissance songs. Not to everyone's liking, perhaps, but it should be quite fine."

Caroline remembered long evenings when she had been alone, Lawrence off heaven knew where, and her only solace was in volumes of poetry by Sir Phillip Sidney and Edmund Spenser. "I adore Renaissance songs."

"Do you? So does Justin. You will both have to explain the songs to me, then. And the next week there is a large assembly planned. You will have to go with us to that, as well. I intend to enjoy your company as long as I can."

Caroline glanced back at Justin. An evening of music and then an assembly in his company—this summer just grew better and better.

She let a small, hopeful feeling into her heart, as she had never dared to before.

Then Lady Bellweather came back from where she examined the mosaics with her younger daughters, and the littlest one sat down on Caroline's lap to show her her doll. All romantic fantasies were lost in the immediate practicalities of getting the doll's tiny boot laced up properly.

Chapter Fourteen

Two days after the picnic excursion, Caroline found herself standing on a dock, staring at a large, bobbing boat.

It is a yacht, she reminded herself. *Not a boat— a yacht.*

But no matter what it was called, it looked terribly precarious, rolling with the waves that slapped at its wooden sides. And she was meant to be climbing aboard for a pleasure excursion.

Pleasure? Ha!

Whatever had she been thinking when she agreed to this? She was not a good sailor at all, and just watching the pitch of the boat—yacht— was making her feel a bit queasy.

Of course you know why you agreed to this outing, her blasted, ever-present inner voice whispered. *It is because the Sewards are the ones who invited you.*

One Seward in particular.

Lord Lyndon. Justin.

She had thought about him a great deal since the picnic, gone over all their conversations, every glance that had passed between them. She felt a bit like a silly schoolgirl, prostrate with calf-love for the music master. She wanted to see him again, talk to him some more, maybe have another moment alone with him.

All of which was a very bad idea. The more she saw him, talked to him, the more she liked him. And the more she felt guilty about deceiving him.

But she could not seem to stay away today. Even if it did mean she had to get on the boat.

"Caro, isn't this fascinating?" Phoebe called, coming around a corner with the grizzled captain of the yacht. She looked jauntily nautical in a blue-and-white dress and matching bonnet. "Captain Jones was just showing me how the boat is moored, and he says I can help steer once we are aboard."

"That is very kind of Captain Jones, Phoebe," Caroline answered with a smile. "I just hope you will not run us aground."

"Of course I shan't! Captain Jones says I am a real sea spaniel."

"Sea *dog*, miss," the old captain corrected.

"Yes, of course! Sea dog." Phoebe looked about happily at the boat and the water, completely in her element.

Caroline hoped her sister would not take it into her head now to find some Navy man and elope with him. Or worse, disguise herself and join the Navy in her own right!

These ruminations were cut short by the sound of Harry Seward calling, "Hallo! Mrs. Aldritch, Miss Lane, you are here already."

Caroline turned to see Harry, Justin, Lady Lyndon, and Sarah Bellweather coming toward them, all of them outfitted for a sea jaunt. Harry carried a large hamper, trying to balance it and wave at the same time.

Phoebe rushed over to greet them, and Caroline followed at a slower pace. Her gaze met Justin's, and he gave her a small smile.

Her breath caught at that small, secret curve of his lips, and she smiled at him in return. She could not seem to help herself.

"The water looks calm today," he said.

Caroline glanced doubtfully at the still-lapping waves. "Do you think so?"

Justin laughed. "Not much of a sailor, eh, Mrs. Aldritch?"

"I'm not sure. I have not had much opportunity for sailing."

"Well, I shall help you, then," he said, a teasing twinkle in his blue eyes. "I often went out on the river in India. I won't let you fall overboard."

Was he *flirting* with her? Caroline looked at him, at his half smile. It had been so long since she had indulged in harmless, lighthearted flirtation that she could scarce remember how it was done.

Finally, she smiled, took his proffered arm, and let him help her climb aboard the waiting yacht. They sat down on a bench near the railing and watched as Phoebe, Harry, and Sarah scrambled onto the deck, laughing and chattering boisterously. Phoebe rushed over to climb up on a coiled pile of rope, pointing and exclaiming over something in the water below.

Harry looked at her with a rapt expression on his face.

Lady Lyndon sat down beside Caroline and Justin on the bench, settling her mulberry-colored skirts about her. "Oh, my dears," she sighed, "I feel so very old just watching them. Was I ever so enthusiastic?"

Caroline nodded in agreement. Once she would

have dashed about just like Phoebe, bursting with the joy, the glee, the possibility of life. But years and experience had killed that feeling, had left her feeling numb. Like an old woman.

Now Justin's arm brushed against hers as he leaned forward to retrieve something from the hamper. And the cold, hard knot at the core of her seemed to burst open, releasing that old joyful feeling again. She almost laughed aloud with the delightful surprise of it.

Then the boat began to move, and she was jolted against his arm. She clutched at his sleeve with her hand, catching the smooth wool in her fist.

Justin's other arm came around to steady her, and she found herself in an almost embrace with him. Everything else, the people, the sea, the rocking of the boat, faded around her. She only saw him.

She looked up at his face, so near hers, and wondered dazedly if his lips were as soft as they looked.

Justin wished, as he had never wished for anything before in his life, that he was alone with Mrs. Aldritch.

He was acutely conscious of every move she made, every word she said. He waited eagerly for every time she would tilt up her head and he could see her face beneath the brim of her lavender silk-lined bonnet.

She laughed at something his mother said, her head at a slight angle that caused one pale strand of hair to brush against her cheek.

It made him want to laugh, as well, even though he had no idea what they were talking of.

Then he heard his mother's words.

". . . and there he was, running down the drive without a stitch on, while his nursemaid chased after him."

Oh, dear Lord. Was she telling that old story about the time he was three years old and went dashing about in the altogether again?

She must be. Mrs. Aldritch was looking at him with mirth sparkling in her dark eyes, one lavender-gloved hand pressed over her mouth, holding in her laughter.

His mother continued. "And all the tenants were walking home from the farm at that hour. I would vow that every single one of them saw that tiny dimple just above—"

"Mother!" Justin interrupted desperately, "I am sure you must be boring Mrs. Aldritch with my childhood exploits. Not to mention how improper it is."

Caroline took her hand away from her mouth and said, "I found it to be an extremely diverting story, Lord Lyndon. Extremely diverting, indeed."

"And you are not one to be lecturing about propriety, Justin," his mother added. "That is the *least* of the stories I could tell about you, my dear. Why, there was the time you and young Harry broke into the wine cellar. . . ."

Justin had the unhappy feeling that this talebearing could go on for hours. He wanted Caroline Aldritch to like him, to be impressed by him. Not think he was some wild 'un who always ran about without his clothes as a child.

He stood up quickly and said, "I do believe you expressed an interest in seeing the, er, wheel, Mrs. Aldritch." Is that what they called the steering mechanism of yachts? A wheel? Justin certainly hoped so. He couldn't afford to look any more foolish.

She looked up at him quizzically, with a half smile that said she knew exactly what he was doing. "Did I? Yes. I would like to see the, er, wheel."

With a last word for his mother, she rose and took his arm, allowing him to lead her along the deck. They went past the three young people, who were watching one of the sailors demonstrate knot making, and stopped in the relatively quiet stern.

Caroline leaned her arms on the rail and looked down at the water below. "You are not fooling me one bit, you know," she said, laughter still lingering in her voice.

Justin also leaned on the rail, inches away from her. "Not fooling you about what?"

"I never asked to see any wheels. You merely did not want me to hear any more of your childhood exploits."

"Guilty as charged," he admitted blithely. "They cannot be very amusing to anyone but my mother."

"Oh, no. I found them vastly amusing."

"Then it is not fair. No one is here to tell tales of *your* childhood, Mrs. Aldritch."

"Indeed not. Phoebe is so much younger that she does not recall much. And a good thing it is, too. I had a dull country childhood."

"Nothing about you could possibly be dull," he said, without thinking.

She looked at him from beneath her bonnet, her expression unreadable. "On the contrary. I am very dull, I assure you." Then she turned from him, leaning her back against the railing while she watched her sister.

Justin sensed her drawing away, pulling back inside herself. He wanted desperately to bring her back, to bring back the lightly teasing woman. But he did not know how.

So he said, "My mother told me she invited you to the concert with us on Saturday."

"Yes. I hope that is quite all right?"

"Certainly. I look forward to it."

"Phoebe is very excited. She has already changed her plans for her ensemble four times!"

"And you, Mrs. Aldritch? Are you excited about the concert?"

She turned back to look at him, but before she could reply a chilly wind swept across the deck, pushing back her bonnet. She clutched at the silk brim and looked about worriedly.

Justin only then noticed that the sky, so blue when they set out, had become overcast. He had been so engrossed in talking with Mrs. Aldritch that everything else had faded about him.

Now he saw the captain coming toward them, trailed by his mother, Harry, Miss Lane, and Miss Bellweather. "It looks as if we might be in for a bit of a shower, my lord," he said. "Might be best if you all went below for a while."

"Is it dangerous?" Mrs. Aldritch asked in a tight voice.

"Not at all, ma'am," the captain answered. "We just wouldn't want you to be getting damp."

Justin offered her his arm again and said in what he hoped was a reassuring tone, "I am sure it is nothing at all, Mrs. Aldritch. Let us go down below, and we can have our luncheon."

She nodded and smiled, but her grasp was hard on his arm.

*   *   *

Caroline did not like this one bit.

It was not a real storm, but the soft sound of rain falling on the deck underlay the merry chatter of the party. The boat rocked gently, causing wine and lemonade to slosh against the sides of glasses.

Her stomach wouldn't allow her to partake of the picnic luncheon spread across a table, and she feared her smile at the others' sallies was rather strained. She had no desire to ruin their fine time, so she was very glad when Phoebe suggested a diversion.

Even if that diversion was a game of cards.

Caroline watched warily as Harry dug a pack of cards from the bottom of the hamper and shuffled them deftly. Just the sight of the brightly colored pasteboards brought back unwelcome memories of the Golden Feather.

She steeled herself against those memories now and forced herself to smile as if she had not a care in the world. *You survived Lady Lyndon's card party,* she told herself sternly. *You will survive this.*

But the card party had felt somewhat different. There had been so very many people about, all of them eminently respectable, and there had been no stakes. This was more intimate, just her, Lord Lyndon, Harry, Phoebe, and Sarah seated around a table, while Lady Lyndon watched.

She felt absurdly as if all eyes were on her, judging, waiting for her to slip.

Then she laughed inwardly at herself. No one was watching her at all! Indeed, Harry and Phoebe were so busy giggling at each other that *they* saw nothing else.

Caroline lightly touched the pile of cards, and said, "What shall we play, then? Whist?"

"Oh, no!" Phoebe cried. "That is far too stodgy for being among friends. Let us play Speculation."

"Jolly good!" said Harry. "I shall be dealer." He proceeded to pass out three cards to each player, then put the card to trump faceup in the center.

And, as Caroline looked down at the cards in her hand, the old coolness she had once known when she played dealer at the Golden Feather stole over her again. It was unbidden and unwelcome, but she knew only one thing—she wanted to win.

Justin watched in wonder as Mrs. Aldritch once again produced the highest trump and took the pot. He thought he had never seen a woman so intent on a friendly game of Speculation before, or so good at strategy and winning. She would stop at nothing to secure the trump card!

"Oh, Caro, you win again," Phoebe said with a laugh. "How very unfair! I had no idea what a cardsharper you are."

Caroline froze in the act of collecting her winnings, her hands suddenly still. She looked at her sister as if she had never seen her before.

"What did you say, Phoebe?" she said quietly.

"I said I had no idea what a cardsharper you are! Why, you have trounced us all. I vow I will never play a quiet game of piquet with you in the evening again."

Phoebe's tone was blithe, but Caroline looked oddly stricken. Justin watched, puzzled, as she pulled her hands back as if burned. She stood up suddenly, her face pale.

"What is the matter, Caro?" Phoebe asked, her bright smile turning to a worried frown. "Are you ill?"

"It is very warm in here," said Justin's mother. "Do you feel faint, my dear?"

Justin rose beside Caroline, reaching out a hand to steady her as she swayed a bit. "Let me pour you some wine, Mrs. Aldritch."

She turned to him as if startled to see him there. "Oh, no, thank you. I-I think I just need some air. If you all will excuse me for a moment."

"Shall I come with you?" Phoebe said, laying down her own cards on the table.

"Oh, no, Phoebe dear. Stay here and enjoy yourself." Caroline gave a vague smile and turned to climb the stairs back to the deck.

Amelia came to Justin and whispered in his ear, "Perhaps you should go with her, Justin. She does not look well."

He nodded and went to follow her up the stairs.

She stood beneath the eaves of the cabin, watching the light rain that still fell. She rubbed at her arms, as if chilled beneath the thin muslin of her lavender-and-white gown, but she didn't seem to notice her actions. Indeed, she didn't seem to notice anything as she stared out at the deck.

Justin removed his coat and slid it over her shoulders.

She started a bit, as if surprised to see him. Then she gave him a regretful, grateful little smile and drew the warm wool of the coat closer about her.

"How foolish you must think me," she murmured.

"Not at all," he answered. "It was rather close in there."

"I don't know what came over me. I suddenly did not feel like myself." She closed her eyes and took a deep breath, turning her face into the brisk breeze. Little droplets of water clung to her eyelashes and cheeks.

Justin wanted to brush them away, to touch the ivory of her cheek and see if it was as soft as it appeared. Instead, he took her arm through the layers of his coat and her gown and led her to one of the benches.

As they sat down there, out of the rain, he had a sudden idea as to what had brought on her odd behavior. "It was the cards, wasn't it?" he said.

"What!" She drew away from him, looking at him with wide eyes. "The cards?"

"Yes. I knew Larry, remember? I know he had . . . difficulties controlling his card playing."

"Oh." She sat back again cautiously. "Perhaps that *was* it."

Justin felt like an utter cad. He should have known that perhaps she disapproved of cards and gambling, even among friends.

And he wondered with a pang if her lovely face would cloud with disapproval if she ever found out what a rake he himself had been, so long ago.

He did not know!

For one agonizing instant, Caroline had feared he knew the truth. When he asked her if it was the cards that had bothered her, she had been sure he had guessed.

She had been very silly to get so caught up in the game. At the Golden Feather, winning had been her business, and she took her games there very seriously indeed. Today, for a brief while, she had forgotten that her life was different now. A friendly game of cards was just that.

She looked at Justin, at his handsome, worried, admiring face. It would be terrible to see that admiration turn to disgust at the truth.

She would not be so foolish as to forget herself again.

"Tell me more about this concert we are to attend on Saturday," she forced herself to say lightly. "I am so looking forward to it."

Chapter Fifteen

" 'When Nature made her chief work, Stella's eyes,
In color black, why wrapp'd she beams so bright?
Would she in beamy black, like painter wise, Frame
daintiest lustre, mix'd of shades and light?' "

As the soprano sang out, Justin looked down at
the woman who sat beside him, her brown eyes
cast down to read her program, and reflected that
the words could have been written about her.

As indeed could all the songs, a cycle based on
Sir Phillip Sidney's *Astrophil and Stella*. Mrs. Aldritch was very like Stella, the star—beautiful, elegant, remote, and out of reach. Every time he
thought he began to understand her, like at the
picnic, she slid out of his grasp again. Like on the
yacht.

She slowly raised her "beamy black" eyes to look
at the soprano, and he was surprised to see that
they were suspiciously bright. Her lips moved gently, molding around the words.

The program trembled in her gloved hands.

She was obviously in a world of her own, made
of the beauty of the language and the imagery of
perfect, elusive love.

" 'Both so and thus, she minding Love should be
Placed ever there, gave him this mourning weed,
To honor all their deaths, who for her bleed.' "

The soprano finished her song amid applause and
stepped back for an intermission.

Mrs. Aldritch wiped quickly at her cheeks with
the tips of her fingers and smiled at him. "Is the
music not beautiful?"

"Exquisite," he said, meaning more than just
the music.

"I have never heard the poems set to music before, but it is very well done. It suits the words
well."

"You know *Astrophil and Stella,* then?"

"Oh, yes! I used to—" She broke off with a
strange little laugh. "That is, when I was younger
I had a great deal of time for reading. Sidney was
a favorite."

Justin grinned at her. "You mean you did not
prefer *Henrietta's Revenge,* as your sister does?"

She grinned back. "I fear not. I have tried to tell
her that Shakespeare and Sidney are full of the
things she loves to read about, but she does not
believe me."

"You mean revenge, curses, and star-crossed
love?"

"Indeed. You are familiar with the Elizabethans,
then, Lord Lyndon?"

"I will tell you a secret, Mrs. Aldritch. I read
them at Cambridge, and adored them. But I did it
secretly. It would never have done for the dons to
know; it would have ruined my reputation as a n'er-
do-well."

She laughed. "Heaven forbid! Then, tell me,

which of the *Astrophil* poems do you prefer? I like 'Some lovers speak, when they their muses entertain.' "

Justin thought for a moment, then, gazing steadily into her eyes, quoted, " 'A strife is grown between Virtue and Love, While each pretends that Stella must be his: Her eyes, her lips, her all, saith Love, do this, Since they do wear his badge, most firmly prove.' "

She watched him with wide, dark eyes, and whispered, " 'But Virtue thus that title doth disprove, that Stella—' "

" 'O dear name that Stella is That virtuous soul, sure heir of heav'nly bliss.' "

They looked at each other in silence, all the chatter and activity around them fading away, leaving them alone on an island of poetry and silence.

Then she broke the spell by giving a small smile, and saying, "Oh, my. You *do* have hidden depths, Lord Lyndon."

"I could say the same of you, Mrs. Aldritch," he answered.

"Indeed you could," she murmured, looking back down at the program. "Indeed you could."

Justin's mother leaned over, from where she sat on Justin's other side. "My dears," she said, "do tell me what is meant when the song says 'Till that good god make church and churchmen starve.' It sounds most unpleasant."

Mrs. Aldritch also leaned forward and launched into a most erudite explanation of Neoplatonic theory. But he heard not a word of it. Her hair brushed against his throat as she leaned forward, and a scent, sweet and exotic at the same time, floated up to him. Jasmine, he thought, breathing it in deeply.

How it reminded him of India! Of warm, thick nights, filled with the rich scent of this same flower and dry earth, and with the sounds of music and chanting.

It suited her perfectly.

Caroline tried to pay strict attention to the singer when the music resumed, but although the song was lovely, her mind kept drifting.

To the man beside her.

His warmth seemed to reach out and curl around her; the scent of his soap was clean and spicy. Every once in a while, as he turned over a page in his program or leaned to whisper a word to his mother, his arm and shoulder would brush against her. The superfine of his sleeve touched, just barely, the half inch of bare skin between her glove and her puffed muslin sleeve; then it slid away.

Caroline opened her painted silk fan and waved it in front of her face, disarranging her carefully made curls. Really, they should ventilate the concert rooms better!

And she should stop mooning over Lord Lyndon. She was far too old to be behaving like a lovestruck schoolgirl; she had more important things to concern herself with.

Such as Phoebe. She looked about until she found her sister, seated at the end of the row with Harry and Sarah. The three of them were whispering and giggling, obviously paying no attention to the music or anything else.

As Caroline watched, Phoebe peeked up at Harry from beneath her lashes and gave him a flirtatious little smile. Harry blushed and grinned.

Caroline frowned.

When she had hoped for a match for Phoebe in Wycombe, Harry Seward was not at all what she had in mind. Far from being a quiet, respectable vicar or squire, Harry was young and wild. She remembered the fight on her last night at the Golden Feather, and grimaced.

Life with Harry would not be the secure one Caroline wanted for her sister.

But then, Phoebe was not exactly quiet herself. Perhaps no calm squire would have her.

"You are frowning, Mrs. Aldritch," Lord Lyndon whispered in her ear, his warm breath stirring the curls at her temple. "Do you disapprove of the song?"

"Not at all," Caroline answered, with one last glance at Phoebe. Then she turned back to smile at him. "It is quite fine."

"But you feel you must keep a stern eye on your sister."

"Can you blame me?"

"Not at all. I have also been watching Harry. But I think we need not fear that they will run away to the shore again. Not after the scoldings we gave them."

"Indeed not! Phoebe was all that was contrite."

Lord Lyndon gave a small sigh. "As was Harry. But it is very wearing, is it not, Mrs. Aldritch, to always have to be the responsible adult?"

Indeed it was. Caroline reflected that if she were still the reckless, romantic girl she had been before she wed Lawrence, she would not be sitting here so quietly. She would be trying to lure Lord Lyndon to the shore.

But that girl was no more. She was buried under the weight of the years of a difficult marriage and the Golden Feather. She had to make certain that Phoebe did not follow the same reckless path she had, and that was all that was important now.

So she just nodded and smiled sympathetically.

Chapter Sixteen

The next several days passed in an idyllic whirl. Caroline and Phoebe spent a great deal of time with the Sewards and the Bellweathers, but they also met many other people in Wycombe for the summer. There were venetian breakfasts, teas, more card parties, a play, a dance, and another, sunnier boating party. There were also warm, convivial afternoons bathing in the sea, and mornings looking in the shops.

There was scarcely time to pause for thought.

But when Caroline *would* have a quiet moment, when bathing or dressing or in bed about to fall asleep, she would think of Justin.

He had been very attentive, sitting beside her at suppers or playing cards at the same table with her (fortunately, there were no more flashbacks to card-playing days at the Golden Feather!). Justin was a charming companion, funny and interesting and always polite.

But he was that way with everyone, from the littlest Bellweather girl to the ancient Lady Ryce. She felt rather foolish wishing, hoping, that his attentions were a mark of admiration for her specifically. Even if they were, she could scarcely afford to encourage them.

That did not mean, though, that she could not dream and imagine, all alone in her room.

And wonder if he would ask her to dance with him at the grand assembly.

The evening of the grand assembly was a very warm one. All the windows in the high-ceilinged assembly rooms were open to admit what little breeze there was, but still the mingled scent of perfumes, flowers, and warm people hung heavy in the air.

Caroline stood close to one of the windows, fanning herself and wishing that her gray silk gown was a little less weighty. She watched as Phoebe, partnered with Harry, moved blithely through the figures of the dance, seemingly immune to the heat in her bright yellow muslin gown. Phoebe's curls, piled fetchingly atop her head and caught with ivory combs, were still crisp, while Caroline feared that her own locks were quite wilted beneath her opal and seed pearl bandeau.

She supposed she really ought to move about, greet the many people she had met under the auspices of Lady Lyndon these last weeks. But the heat, combined with her sleepless night and the thoughts of Justin that caused it, made her feet feel leaden in their satin slippers. Her mind was dull and languid.

She leaned back against the window frame and wished she could go outside and search for some fresh air.

"Would you care for some lemonade, Mrs. Aldritch?" a familiar voice said. The voice that had echoed in her mind all the night before, keeping her awake.

Caroline turned to see Justin standing there, two glasses of the pale yellow liquid in his hands.

He smiled at her tentatively. "I do hope I didn't startle you."

"Oh, no. I was just . . . thinking," she answered, managing to summon up a small smile in return. She took the offered glass and sipped at the cool lemonade gratefully. The tang of it seemed to help clear her mind a bit. "Thank you. This is delicious."

He leaned against the wall beside her, drinking from his own glass. "I always thought that the seaside was meant to be cool. But if I closed my eyes now, I might almost imagine myself in India again."

"It does seem rather foolish of us to truss ourselves up in silk and go out dancing on such an evening," Caroline said with a laugh.

"I do not see you dancing," Justin teased.

"Nor I you. It must be because we are too sensible."

"Unlike our siblings, you mean?"

They watched as Harry and Phoebe skipped down the line of the dance, ending their set with a bow and a curtsy. Phoebe was quickly claimed by her next partner, and Harry went off to sit with his mother and watch Phoebe. The music for the next set, an old-fashioned minuet, struck up.

"I suppose, then," Justin continued, "that since we are so sensible, it would be futile for me to ask you to dance."

Actually, despite the heat, Caroline could think of nothing she would like better. To feel his hand on hers, his grasp at her waist, would be everything she longed for.

Well . . . almost everything.

And it would be so dangerous.

"I fear I must decline," she answered, hoping her tone was light and teasing. "Not that you would make such a poor partner, I'm sure! But I can summon little enthusiasm for the exercise this evening."

"How about a stroll on the terrace, then? Perhaps we could find a breeze out there."

The thought of fresh air, not to mention the thought of Justin at her side, almost alone, was too much temptation to bear.

She gave in to that temptation and nodded. "I would like that, thank you."

Justin placed their empty glasses on a table and offered her his arm. Caroline glanced over to make certain Phoebe was well-occupied, then slid her hand over the soft cloth of his sleeve. She seemed to have no control over her feet; the satin slippers led her inexorably out the doors into the night, even as she told them how foolish they were being, in light of her feelings for Lyndon. It seemed the height of folly to be alone with him in the night.

But they were not entirely alone. A few other couples had come outside in search of a cool breeze and stood along the marble balustrade talking and looking out at the sea. Justin and Caroline walked along until they came to the end of the terrace, where it was quiet and dark, except for the bars of light and faint music that came from the window.

Caroline stepped into the shadows and turned her face to the light breeze from the sea.

"Mother has been saying we should go soon to Waring Castle," Justin said softly.

Caroline looked at him. His face was half in shadow, and he watched the water.

"Your country estate?" she said.

"Yes. She does not want to go; she is quite loath to quit Wycombe. But I have not been to Waring since I returned to England, and it is past time to see to my duty."

"Of course. Will you go soon?"

"Perhaps in a fortnight; not sooner. The Bellweathers are thinking of going to Brighton then, and Mother won't want to leave while they are still here."

A fortnight. Caroline closed her eyes against the sudden rush of ineffable sadness. In only fourteen days the idyllic summer of picnics, boating, concerts, and suppers would be at an end. Justin and his family would be gone, vanished into their world of duty, and she and Phoebe would be at loose ends again.

She did not want to lose it all, she realized with a fierce pang. She didn't want to lose that feeling of respectability, of belonging that the summer had brought. She didn't want to lose dear Lady Lyndon's friendship, or the chance to laugh at Harry's ridiculous antics, or play at dolls with the little Bellweather girls.

Above all, she did not want to lose Justin. Their conversations, the times she was in his company, had come to mean so much.

They meant all the world.

She had done what she swore she would never do—she had fallen in love. With Justin. Lord Lyndon. The one man who could expose her for the terrible fraud she was.

"Phoebe and I will . . . will miss you terribly,"

she managed to choke out, when all she really wanted to do was run away and hide, to cry alone like a wounded animal.

"I know that Harry will miss your sister. To be honest, I think he means to make her an offer before we go. But I have been thinking he should go to oversee another estate of ours, Seward Park, and grow up a bit before he takes on such responsibility."

Caroline nodded. "I did fear that. Not that you would send him away, that he would make her an offer."

"Feared?"

"Yes. You are being honest, Lord Lyndon, so I will be as well. Once, all I could have wished for Phoebe would be to marry someone from a family like yours. It would be a great honor for her. But I see now that even though she is of an age to wed, she is too young in her feelings. I would be doing her a great disservice to let her make the same mistake I did."

"You married too young?"

"Oh, yes. So I think you are wise to give Harry some task far away. Phoebe and I will travel for a year, maybe come to London for the Season. Perhaps then, if your brother were to meet us again, things would be different. If you had no objections?"

"How could I? Harry would be lucky to win your sister. Miss Lane is charming." He paused, then went on in an oddly thick voice. "But not quite as charming as you."

Caroline looked up at him, confused. Could he possibly? . . .

No. He could not be feeling the same way she was.

But his gaze was intense as he looked at her, his eyes almost silver in the meager light.

Inside, the orchestra began a waltz, and its lilting strains floated out to them on the night wind.

"Would you care to dance?" he asked.

Wordlessly, Caroline nodded. The heat of the evening no longer seemed to matter, for she craved the warmth of Justin's touch.

He slid his arm about her waist, warm and secure through the silk of her gown. She made the automatic motions of sweeping up her short train in one hand and sliding the other into his.

His fingers closed about hers tightly, and they began to move. Unmindful of anyone who might be watching, they swayed and turned about their small patch of marble.

Closer than was strictly proper, their bodies moved together as if they had been dancing thus for years. His legs brushed against the silk of her skirts, and the fabric clung to him, as Caroline longed to do herself.

Slowly, they twirled to a halt at the edge of the terrace, alone in the darkest shadows. Caroline stared up at him, as breathless as if she had run a mile. Her heart was full, so full she feared it might burst.

He looked down at her, his lips parted as if he were about to say something but could not find the words. Then he *did* find the words.

"Mrs. Aldritch," he whispered, "I do believe I love you."

And Caroline's heart *did* burst. She could feel the tears welling up in her eyes and falling down her cheeks, but she could not let go of him to brush them away. She had been alone, lonely, for so long. She needed his closeness, his touch. Only his. Justin's.

"I think," she whispered back, "that you should call me Caroline."

Caroline, Justin's mind sang. *Caroline, Caroline.* He looked at her in the moonlight and thought he had never seen a more beautiful sight. She almost glowed, as if she were made of the finest marble, the most expensive alabaster.

"Caroline," he whispered. Only that. But all his heart was in that one word.

Caroline.

She must have heard all the ache, all the longing in his voice, for her lips parted in an expression of wonder. "Justin," she whispered. "Justin."

He glanced quickly behind them. Everyone who was on the terrace had gone back inside to join the waltz, but the windows all stood open.

"Walk with me in the garden," he urged.

"I . . ." She looked around uncertainly. "I should look in on Phoebe."

"My mother is no doubt watching her. It will only be for a moment. Please."

She nodded and walked with him down the terrace steps into the small garden adjacent to the sea. Once they were outside the light, he slid his arm about her waist. She leaned against him, her pale hair brushing against the shoulder of his coat.

They stopped beneath the sheltering branches of a tree, and Caroline turned to face him.

"Did I shock you with my words of love?" he asked.

She shook her head. "It has been a long time

since I was shocked by anything. Though I was rather surprised. We have not known each other very long."

"Does that mean that you do not return my feelings? You know you need only say the word and I will bother you no more."

She gave him a little half smile. "Bother me? Silly man. Don't you know that I love you, too?"

Joy unlike any he had ever known blossomed in Justin's tired heart. Joy and another unfamiliar emotion.

Hope.

Hope for the future, for a happy life, a family of his own. With this woman, who was so unlike anyone he had ever met before, all things seemed possible.

In a burst of emotion, he pulled her closer to him and lowered his lips to hers.

Her mouth was soft and cool, and it yielded so sweetly, so perfectly beneath his. He felt her rise up on tiptoes and slide her arms about his shoulders, her fingers tangling in his hair.

The kiss, so gently begun, caught fire. Justin drew her even closer, urged her lips to part under his passion.

She responded, clinging to him, mingling her sighs, her soft moans, with his.

Suddenly, he knew that if they went on this way he would not be able to stop with a kiss. He would not be able to let her go all night.

He pulled away from her slowly and dragged in long, ragged breaths of warm night air. Her forehead fell to his shoulder, and he felt her slim frame tremble under his hands.

He held her away a bit and saw tears on her cheeks, shimmering in the moonlight. "Caroline!" he cried, shocked at this reaction to his kiss. Was he so terribly out of practice, then? "What is wrong?"

She shook her head and wiped away the teardrops with her gloved hand. "It is just that I am so happy. I have never felt this way before, ever. It is too wonderful. Too wonderful to last."

He drew her back against him, holding her very tightly. So tightly he could vow he felt her heart beat against his chest. He rested his cheek against the silk of her hair and closed his eyes.

"Of course it will last," he said firmly. "Of course it will."

Her grip tightened, crushing the fabric of his coat. "Justin, promise me that, no matter what, you will always remember this night, this perfect, perfect night. And remember that I love you with all my heart."

"I shall have to remember it, won't I? To tell our grandchildren someday."

She gave an oddly hysterical little laugh and answered, "Yes." Her voice turned suddenly sad, as if she knew a secret that he did not. "Yes."

Late that night, after the assembly was over and everyone else was abed, Justin sat in his library, staring out the window at the waning moon.

The same moon he had kissed Caroline Aldritch under.

It had been a glorious kiss, the most wonderful, the most intimate of his life. It had felt almost as if he held the very essence of her in his arms and shared himself with her in a way he had never done with anyone else.

And she had seemed to feel it, too. But then she had pulled away, her face sad and strangely bitter.

She said she loved him. But did she then change her mind?

He longed to see her again, right that moment. The wild boy he had once been would have gone to her house and climbed up to her window, demanded to know the truth of what was in her mind, in her heart.

The respectable earl he was now knew he would have to wait until the next day to see her, to talk to her. But it felt like a hundred years until daylight.

Caroline also lay awake in her bed, listening to the distant sounds of the sea whispering through her open window. Her scarred ankle itched, and as she reached down to rub it she thought about the moments in the garden, going over each one carefully, minutely.

They had been the most perfect moments of her life, and she wanted to memorize each one, tuck them close, and hold them forever. For she knew it could not last.

Justin truly loved her. She did believe that. He understood her, understood her struggles, as she understood him. But she could not be with him. Once he knew the truth about the Golden Feather and Mrs. Archer, he would look at her very differently. He might understand the forces that had led her along that path, but he had a family, a title, and a position to uphold.

Yes, he might now be talking about the grand-children they would have together, but he would not be after he found out about her past.

And she knew, as surely as she knew she loved him, that she would have to tell him. Soon.

Chapter Seventeen

"What shall we do today, Caro?" Phoebe asked, stretching out on a chaise set in a patch of morning sunlight. She looked like a satisfied little cat, lazy after the dancing and talking of the night before.

Caroline looked up from the book she was ostensibly reading. In truth, she had not turned a page in fully fifteen minutes; she was too caught up in thoughts of Justin to concentrate. "Whatever you like, I suppose, dearest. We have no engagements until the Westons' supper this evening. Would you want to go to the shops?"

Phoebe wrinkled her nose. "It is too warm to shop. Last night I thought I would faint for lack of air in the assembly rooms."

"You seemed to be having a fine time."

"Oh, I was! Anytime I can dance is a fine time." She slid Caroline a sly glance. "I noticed you quite vanished before the supper."

Caroline looked back down at her book. "I was in need of some air."

"Ah, yes. Apparently so was Lord Lyndon." Phoebe leaned forward eagerly. "Is there anything you want to tell your sister, Caro? Anything at all?"

Tell Phoebe that she kissed Lord Lyndon in the moonlight, but she couldn't marry him because she had once been the proprietor of a gaming hell? Caroline thought not.

"I did happen to stroll with him on the terrace for a while," she answered carefully. "But there is no need to act like this is scene from one of your novels, Phoebe. There were many other people there, and . . . and nothing of any consequence happened."

"Nothing at all?"

She just lost her heart, that was all. "Nothing."

Phoebe fell back with a disappointed little huff. "How very vexing. I was hoping this would be a *romantic* summer."

Caroline laughed at her pouting expression. "I believe you have enough romance for the both of us. This house is flooded with bouquets from your admirers every day."

Phoebe tried to shrug carelessly, but she looked too pleased for it to be effective. "But that is not really romance!"

"It isn't? Then what is?"

"Grand emotion! Passionate declarations! Embraces under the stars!" She peered closer at Caroline. "Did you and Lord Lyndon embrace under the stars?"

Caroline laughed harder. "Phoebe!"

"No? Well, you should have."

Caroline decided that a small fib might be in order. "We did not 'embrace under the stars.' And you and young Mr. Seward had best not have done so, either."

"Oh, Harry Seward. All he has talked of these last few days is 'making a name for himself' and 'having adventures.' Nothing romantic at all. I don't know what has gotten into him.''

Caroline nodded. She remembered Justin saying he wanted to send Harry to manage one of the family's smaller estates, but she would have thought Harry would not be very enthusiastic about it. Perhaps she had been wrong, and he liked the idea of his independence.

"Are you disappointed in him, then, Phoebe?" she asked.

Phoebe shook her head firmly, but her violet-blue eyes looked a bit sad. "What is there to be disappointed in? He is a silly young man, not at all like the Count Enrico in *The Sins of Madame Sophie*. Beside, I have adventures of my own to have! Starting today." She gave a dramatic little pause. "Let's go bathing."

Caroline closed her book, glad to have a purpose for the day besides brooding over Justin. "An excellent idea! But I am sure everyone else in town will want to do the same. Perhaps I should send Mary to reserve a bathing house."

"No need for that! Sarah Bellweather showed me the most delightful cove, just outside of town. It's very quiet there; not many people know about it. If we went there to bathe, we wouldn't have to worry about bathing houses and crowds. We would be all alone." Phoebe giggled. "We could even take off our stockings!"

"I hardly think *that* would be appropriate," Caroline murmured. But a quiet swim, just the two of them and the sea and the sky, with no crowds, sounded just what she needed. "We could go there, though, and take a picnic."

"Wonderful! I'll just go change into my bathing

costume, then." Phoebe rushed off, calling for Mary to come and help her dress.

Caroline set aside her book with a pang of guilty relief. If she was bathing with Phoebe all day, she couldn't call on Justin with her tale of the Golden Feather until tomorrow. Or the next day. Perhaps that was just as well. She needed time to gather her thoughts, prepare her words very carefully. She didn't want to hurt him, or herself, but he deserved the truth.

"I think, my dears, that I will not go with you to Waring," Lady Lyndon announced at breakfast the morning after the assembly.

Justin turned to his mother in surprise. "I thought you *wanted* to go to Waring, Mother."

"Oh, I do, and I *will* go there, in the autumn perhaps. But Lady Bellweather has asked me to accompany them to Brighton for the remainder of the summer. I would like that, I think. It has been a long time since I went to Brighton." She touched her napkin to her lips and smiled at them. "But you must go to Waring, of course. You have been away too long, Justin, and the country air will be good for you."

Harry swallowed his bite of eggs and said, "If Mother isn't going to Waring, then neither am I."

Justin looked at his brother. "And what are you going to do instead? Stay here to dangle after Miss Lane?"

Harry's face took on a rather comically serious expression, and he tilted up his chin. "Certainly not. You mentioned the possibility of my going to manage Seward Park."

"I did, but you hardly seemed enraptured at the possibility."

"Well, that was then. I have given it some thought. I do . . . like Miss Lane, but you were quite right when you said I don't have very much to offer her. If I managed Seward Park very well, then it would prove to her and her sister that I'm not just a useless fribble."

Justin regarded his brother with near shock. For once there was no pouting, no whining on Harry's part. He looked earnest and worried and very, very young. "Harry, that is the first sensible thing I have heard you say since I returned to England."

Harry looked down at his plate, his cheeks reddening. "Yes, well, Miss Lane is a very special young lady. I want to be worthy of her."

"Then you can go to Seward Park. If you make a go of it, then I will give it to you as a wedding present," Justin answered.

"Would you?" Harry cried, his eyes shining with new hope. "You *are* a good 'un, Justin."

Amelia beamed at her sons. "You see, my dears, I knew all would be well!"

The butler came into the breakfast room, carrying a note on a silver tray. "This just came for you, my lord."

"Thank you, Richards." Justin broke the wax seal and read the scrawled words quickly.

"What is it, Justin?" Amelia asked worriedly. "Bad news?"

"Not at all," Justin said with a smile. "It is from next door."

Amelia gave a sly, satisfied smile. "From Mrs. Aldritch?"

"No, from the young lady we were just speaking of. Miss Lane."

"Miss Lane!" Harry cried, half rising from his chair. "Why is she writing to *you*?"

"Now, don't get all upset, Harry. You've been doing so very well this morning. She simply wants to invite us to a picnic at the cove just outside of town."

Harry settled back warily. "Both of us?"

"Of course. She says her sister and Sarah Bellweather will be there, as well."

"That's all right, then. Sounds like jolly fun." Harry popped another bite of eggs into his mouth and chewed happily. "I can wear my new waistcoat, the one embroidered with tulips. She's sure to admire that!"

Justin folded the note back carefully and tucked it beside his plate. It *did* sound like "jolly fun," but he couldn't help the nagging feeling of doubt that crawled inside of him. Why would Miss Lane write the note, and not her older sister? And why the cove, not the more public shore area?

Very strange, indeed. But he would go, of course. He couldn't stay away from Caroline.

He smiled as he remembered their embrace in the night-dark garden. It had been sweet and fiery and perfect. So perfect. Not even her strange sadness after could mar the memory.

He wanted to see her again, to hold her in his arms, to talk to her and tell her all he was feeling.

Why, then, did he have the nagging thought that he should not go on the picnic today?

Chapter Eighteen

"This is wonderful! I feel just like a mermaid." Phoebe splashed about happily in the cool water, her blond hair sleek in the sunlight. She had long ago removed her cap, and now she and Sarah were frolicking like two little seals.

Caroline, perched on an outcropping of rocks with her stockinged toes dangling in the water, laughed when Phoebe splashed her. "You look like a monkey! You will catch a chill without your cap."

"Of course I won't! The water is quite warm. Why don't you come in, Caro?"

"I will in a minute. I want to enjoy the sun first."

Phoebe nodded and went back to swimming in circles with Sarah.

Caroline leaned back on her elbows and closed her eyes to bask in the warm light. She knew she should not; the sun was sure to make her quite brown since she wasn't wearing a hat. But somehow she felt too languid to even worry about her complexion.

The sun, the sounds of the sea and the girls' laughter, and the late night at the assembly all conspired to make her drowsy. She closed her eyes, letting the peace of the moment, so precious and transitory, steal over her.

She was startled into full awakening by the sound of a man's voice calling out.

She looked over her shoulder to see Justin and Harry coming toward them. She sat straight up, automatically tucking her legs beneath her to hide the stockings of her bathing ensemble.

Whatever were *they* doing here, in this out-of-the-way spot? Surely Phoebe would not . . .

"Hello, Lord Lyndon! Mr. Seward!" Phoebe called out, waving her hands from the water, confirming Caroline's sudden suspicions. "There you are at last."

Caroline gave her a stern glance, but Phoebe just smiled blithely and swam over to snatch her cap and stockings up from where she left them on the rocks. She donned them beneath the water and came out onto the shore, Sarah behind her.

Caroline stood up and caught Phoebe's arm as she walked past. "Did you invite them here?" she whispered.

"Of course," Phoebe answered innocently. "I thought they might enjoy a picnic. Did I do something wrong, Caro?"

Caroline watched as Justin came closer and closer. He was dressed casually today, in a blue coat, buckskin breeches, and a plain, simply tied cravat. He wore no hat, and the breeze ruffled his sun-touched hair.

He smiled at her and waved.

Caroline thought he was the loveliest sight she had ever seen.

As he came ever closer, she reached up nervously to make certain her hair was still tidy and smooth beneath her cap.

"Good afternoon, ladies," he said, handing Caroline a small parcel. "Mother sent some of her raspberry cordial, since she couldn't be with us today."

Caroline stared up at him and heard herself saying, as if from a long way away, "Thank you, Lord Lyndon. We are very glad you and Mr. Seward could come."

"I got the distinct impression earlier that you were rather startled to see us. Did your sister invite us without your knowledge?"

Caroline's hand tightened on Justin's arm. They were walking along the shore after the long and very merry picnic luncheon, watching the three young people where they dug about in the sand up ahead. Looking for smugglers' treasure, no doubt. Then the three of them ran off behind a small hill, out of sight.

"I confess she did," she answered. "But that does not mean that your presence was at all unwelcome. It has been a delightful day."

She realized that these were not just polite words. It *had* been a delightful day, full of laughter and good cheer. She felt warm and happy, with the cordial in her veins, the sun on her head, and Justin beside her.

It was a perfect day, almost as perfect as the night in the assembly rooms garden had been. A day she wished could go on forever and ever.

But she knew it could not.

She turned to face Justin, walking half sideways. "Lord Lyndon—Justin—there is something we have to talk about."

He smiled at her, so sweetly that she felt her resolve to be honest and truthful melting away beneath it until it was almost gone.

Almost.

"I know," he said. "We have many things to talk about. What would you care to start with?"

She tried to steel her resolve against his teasing. His casual, happy manner only made her fear what she must say even more.

She didn't want to lose this, his smile, his laughter, his admiration. She closed her eyes tightly, hoping that not seeing his face would help her to say what she had to say.

Unfortunately, shutting one's eyes while walking is not the wisest thing to do. Her slippered foot caught on a clump of driftwood, and she fell with a thud to the hard-packed sand.

For one moment, she lay there absolutely stunned, unable to move or breathe. She felt sick to her stomach.

Then she felt absolutely mortified. When she finally caught her breath, reality returned, and she realized she was lying like a beached fish at the feet of the man she loved.

She groaned and pressed her forehead harder into the itchy sand. So what if she had been about to destroy his faith in her forever with her confession? That didn't mean she wanted his last vision of her to be *this*. A small part of her, the part that had once been young and foolish and read cheap novels, had wanted him to remember her as tragic, self-sacrificing, and nobly alluring, even as she gave him up.

Well, now she could bid farewell to nobly alluring. He would surely always remember her as awkward and dirty with wet sand.

She moaned softly.

Then she noticed that he was kneeling beside her, calling her name frantically. Her ears must be full of sand, too.

"Caroline!" he cried. "Caroline, can you hear me? Are you conscious?"

She slowly turned her head to look at him, or rather at his arm as he reached for her. She still couldn't bring herself to look at his face. "I am . . . conscious," she murmured.

"Thank the Lord! Are you in pain anywhere? Can you sit up?"

She did ache a bit, but she knew she could not just go on lying there forever. The sand was beginning to prickle. She nodded, and he slid his arms about her, pulling her gently upright.

A sharp pain shot up her left leg, and she cried out.

"What is it?" Justin asked, his blue eyes slate-gray with worry.

"My ankle," she gasped through the throbbing ache. "I must have twisted it when I fell."

"It could be broken."

Caroline shook her head and reached into the tight sleeve of her bathing dress for a handkerchief to wipe her face with. She might be crippled now, but she wanted to be a cripple with a clean face.

"No," she said. "I don't think so."

"We should make certain. Then we will get you to a physician. Where are those blasted children at? They're never about when you actually need them." He reached for her foot and started to draw the heavy woolen stocking down from her knee.

At first, Caroline was too busy scrubbing at her face to truly realize what he was about. Then she felt the soft, tantalizing brush of fingertips against her calf and looked down at him.

For one long moment, time seemed suspended. She could still feel the touch of him on her skin, the sunlight beating down on her head, the piercing ache of her ankle. But she could not move or speak. She was frozen.

Only one image kept replaying itself in her mind. The image of her standing in her office at the Golden Feather while he held her scarred ankle in his hand.

It was an image eerily like the one she was living now. Only now it was so very much worse, because she knew all that she was losing.

And the only thing she could do was watch and wait.

He rolled the stocking to her ankle, then glanced up at her. She made her face as cool and expressionless as she could, and gave him a small nod.

If this was how it was fated to be, then so be it. Perhaps it would be easier if he hated her as a deceiver, after all.

He drew the stocking the rest of the way off and pressed his thumbs to the delicate bones of her foot. They moved gently over the arch, pressing lightly. Closer his touch came, ever closer, until his thumb brushed over the rough, raised scar on her ankle.

Then he stilled. He became as frozen as she herself felt, and even his hands felt chilled against her skin.

He lifted her foot a bit and stared at the pink scar. Caroline fought the urge to yank her foot away, to scream and cry out and run away. She made herself sit there, as still as ice, her face the cool mask she had learned to don in her lonely years at the Golden Feather.

She only wished she had one of her cloth masks to hide behind, as well.

He raised his gaze to hers. His eyes were bewildered and dazed. "How could? . . . Is this? . . ." he said hoarsely. His grasp tightened.

Caroline swallowed hard. "Yes. I am, or was, Mrs. Archer."

Justin slowly placed her foot back onto the sand. Caroline caught up the stocking and pulled it quickly back over her leg, wincing as it passed over the swollen ankle.

The pain was as nothing compared to the pain in her heart.

Justin sat back against the driftwood. The stunned look on his face ripped at her soul. "Tell me," he said.

"What is there to tell? Lawrence died without a farthing to his name. His only legacy to me was the deed to a gaming establishment, a place called the Golden Feather. He won it, you see, in a game of chance the very night he died. So he did not have time to lose it again."

"And you took the place over?"

Caroline nodded wearily. She found she could not go into all the reasons for that action now. She was tired and in pain, and all that seemed so far away now. As if it had all happened to another woman.

Besides, to Justin, a gentleman, her reasons would not matter. A true lady would have chosen genteel poverty over ill-gotten riches.

As indeed she would have, for herself. But not for Phoebe. Never for Phoebe.

And now they were both ruined.

"Why did you not tell me?" he said, his voice tight with anger. "All these weeks, we have spent so much time together, and you never said a word."

"Why do you think I did not tell you? Because then you would have given us the cut direct and made your mother and brother cut us, too. All of Society would have followed your example, starting with the Bellweathers. I could not have borne that for Phoebe, never!"

Caroline feared she was about to start weeping. She turned her face away from him, refusing to look at his furious, wounded eyes any longer.

He stared at her in the heavy silence, his gaze like a hundred knives stabbing at her heart.

Then the dark spell was broken by a piercing shriek.

Caroline looked up to see Phoebe running toward them, closely followed by Harry and Sarah. She had lost her cap again, and her hair fell down in unruly curls. Her hands were bunched into fists, and she was frowning most fiercely. She looked like a vengeful little Valkyrie.

"Once again your guard comes to your rescue," Justin muttered. "First your maid and her book, and now this, Mrs. Aldritch. Mrs. Archer." He raked a shaking hand through his hair, leaving it sticking up in wavy tufts. "Whoever you are."

"I am Caroline," she whispered. "I am me."

But he did not hear her. Phoebe was upon them, shouting, "What have you done to my sister? Why is she sitting in the sand like that? Did you knock her down?"

Justin stared at Phoebe unseeingly. Then he said, "Pardon me. I must . . . go. I am sorry. Harry, please see the ladies home."

Then he stood up and walked quickly down the shore, out of their view.

Caroline watched him until he disappeared, and at that moment she could no longer help herself. The tears she had choked back, making her throat ache, came out in a great salty flood. They fell off her chin and dripped onto her clenched hands.

They were not ladylike, diamondlike tears. They were great, gulping, ugly sobs.

She had not cried like this since she was a little child. Now she could not stop, even though she knew she was creating a scene.

Phoebe and Sarah knelt beside her, patting her and murmuring soothing words. Sarah pulled out a bottle of smelling salts.

Harry fluttered about helplessly, offering hand-kerchiefs and saying in a quavering voice, "Oh, I say! Do let me see you ladies home or send for the physician. Or something. Anything!"

Phoebe glared up at him. "It was *your* brother who caused this, Mr. Seward!"

"No, it wasn't," Caroline protested through her tears. "I caused it. Every bit of it."

"Of course you didn't," Phoebe soothed. "It was Lord Lyndon. Men are such beasts."

"I beg your pardon!" Harry cried.

"Beasts!" Phoebe repeated loudly. She put her arm around Caroline's shoulder and said, "Come, dear, let me take you home."

"*I'll* see you ladies home," Harry offered again.

"We have our own carriage, thank you, Mr. Seward." Phoebe and Sarah helped Caroline up between them and supported her on her injured ankle as they left the sandy shore.

Harry trotted along behind them all the way.

Chapter Nineteen

Justin hardly knew where he was walking. He only knew he had to get away, to escape from the nightmare his life had suddenly become.

He walked blindly down the shore, unaware of the waves lapping at his boots or the birds wheeling overhead. He rubbed his hand hard over his brow, but he could not blot out the vision of Caroline, Mrs. Aldritch/Archer, staring at him with wide, dark eyes in her pale face.

What a blasted, stupid fool he had been not to see what was right before him all these weeks! Of course he recognized Caroline when he first met her, but not because of some mystical union of souls. It was because he had called on her once in her very own gaming house.

She must have laughed at him so behind her hand. The fool who didn't recognize her, who hung about all the time like a love-struck puppy. How easily he had fallen in with her, let her use him for her social ends.

Justin sat down on a large chunk of wood to stare out at the sea, at the white-capped waves that danced and flowed endlessly. He knew it had been insufferably rude of him to leave her and the others alone on the shore, but he *had* to get out of there, to be alone. To think.

He had thought of himself as much changed by his years in India—older and wiser. In truth, he was as silly as Harry, taken in by a pretty face and a sad air.

What a fine actress she was. Her talents were wasted in owning a gaming house, and especially in matronly respectability. She should be treading the boards.

He picked up a stick of wood and tossed it into the water, watching it sink beneath the waves. He should have been thinking of the future all these weeks. He should have followed his mother's original advice and courted and married Miss Bellweather, even if she did prefer digging about in the dirt to matrimony. She never would have made him feel this way, angry and hollow inside.

Because he had truly fallen in love with Caroline, whoever she was. He had never given his heart to any woman like this before, but she touched him with her quiet grace and understanding. He had wanted to take away the sadness in her eyes, to make her life full of nothing but happiness.

It had all been false. All a lie.

But even as he castigated himself for a fool, he could not forget the way she had looked under the moonlight while he kissed her.

"Tell me, Caro, please! Tell me what happened," Phoebe beseeched. She sat on a chair in Caroline's bedroom, watching helplessly as her sister lay in bed, tears still trickling down her cheeks.

Caroline shook her head. She didn't want to talk about what had happened, or anything else. She just wanted to stay here in bed and forget. As if she would ever be able to forget at all. She would see Justin's shocked, betrayed face in her mind forever.

She rolled onto her side to stare out the window. She could just barely see the edge of the house next door.

"At least let Mary and me help you into your nightdress," Phoebe said desperately.

Caroline looked down at herself to see that she still wore her sandy bathing costume. She sat up and reached down to pull at her stockings, taking them off and throwing them onto the floor.

Her scarred ankle was still there. It hadn't been erased.

Phoebe gasped. "Caro, you're hurt! Did Lord Lyndon do that?"

"Of course not. It is an old scar." Caroline rubbed at it furiously with her palm, wishing that it would vanish, and with it all the past.

Her fingernails scraped across the swollen skin there, making it bleed.

Mary, who had just come into the room with a glass of brandy-laced milk, cried out, "Stop that, madam! You are making your injury worse." She rushed over to pull Caroline's hand away and look at the scratches.

"It cannot get any worse," Caroline murmured. "It's all over."

Phoebe's eyes were as wide as saucers. "Caro, you are scaring me. You are acting just like that Lady Macbeth."

Caroline looked over at her, a faint beam of surprise penetrating the fog of her mind. "Lady Macbeth?"

"Well, don't look at me like that. I do sometimes read things other than novels, you know. I am not completely ignorant."

Caroline laughed at that, and Phoebe and Mary exchanged relieved glances.

"Miss Phoebe, go and fetch some warm water and bandages," Mary instructed. "And you, madam, will change out of those dirty clothes and drink every drop of this milk. It will help you rest."

Caroline obediently stood up and unbuttoned the top of her bodice. "I can't rest now. We have to start packing."

"Packing? Where are we going?"

"I don't know. Italy maybe, or America. Somewhere far away." Caroline dropped the last of her clothes and turned back to look at her reflection in the mirror. She looked thin and pale in her chemise, almost like the ghost she felt. "Something terrible has happened, Mary. We are ruined."

And her heart was shattered.

"Ruined, madam?" Mary's voice held only mild curiosity. After four years at the Golden Feather with her mistress, she could hardly be shocked anymore. She dropped a clean nightdress over Caroline's head.

The soft cotton folds enveloped her, sheltering her. "Yes. Justin—Lord Lyndon—discovered the truth about Mrs. Archer."

Now Mary *did* look shocked. Her hands froze on the pearl button she was fastening at Caroline's throat. "Oh, no, madam. Did he threaten to expose you?"

"Not exactly." He had not said much of anything. That was the worst part. If he had shouted, she could have shouted back. But he had just walked away. "You know he *will* tell, though. We will no longer be accepted into the Sewards' house, and people will want to know why."

"Oh, madam!" Mary cried, her lower lip trembling. "I thought we were going to be *normal* now."

"I thought, so, too. But it seems my life is doomed to drama, no matter how much I might wish it otherwise." Caroline pulled a valise out from under the bed and limped to the wardrobe, not even noticing the pain in her ankle as she reached in for an armload of clothes. "I want Phoebe to be affected by this as little as possible, so we must leave at once. Tonight, if possible."

She balled up a lacy petticoat and thrust it into the valise. Then she picked up a pink silk spencer.

"Here, let me do that! You are wrinkling everything." Mary caught the spencer out of Caroline's trembling hands and folded it neatly. "If we have to leave, then we have to leave. You know I will follow you anywhere. Though I must say I do like it here in Wycombe."

"So do I, Mary," Caroline answered wistfully, sitting back down on the bed.

She had never been so happy anywhere in her life before.

Phoebe appeared with a basin of water, which she almost dropped when she saw the open valise. "What are you doing? Where are we going?"

Caroline turned to her sister and held out her hand. "Phoebe, darling, come over here and sit down beside me, so we may talk."

Phoebe backed up, water sloshing from the basin onto her bright green muslin gown. "It's Lord Lyndon, isn't it? He hurt you, and now we must leave to get away from him! How vile he is. I should not have invited him to our outing; then none of this would have happened."

"It isn't like that at all." Caroline had thought to make up some tale for Phoebe about why they were leaving Wycombe. But now, as she looked into her sister's desperate eyes, she knew she had to tell her the truth. She was done forever with lies and half-truths. All they had ever brought her was pain.

Caroline took the basin from Phoebe and placed it carefully on a table. Then she drew her over to sit down on the window seat. She pulled the curtains against the sight of the Sewards' house.

"Now, Phoebe," she said, taking Phoebe's trembling hands in her own, "I must tell you something. We *are* leaving because of Lord Lyndon, but it is not his fault. It is mine."

"Yours, Caro? How can that be?"

Caroline took a deep breath and plunged ahead. "After Lawrence died, I told you I was working as companion to his elderly aunt. Remember?"

"Yes. That is why we could only see each other a couple of times a year."

"I fear I lied to you."

Phoebe looked confused. "Do you mean you were not working for Mr. Aldritch's aunt?"

"No." Caroline closed her eyes so she could not see her sister's reaction to her words. "I-I owned a gaming establishment, called the Golden Feather. Lawrence won it in a game of chance right before he died, and I took it over."

She steeled herself for the storm, for Phoebe to rail at her for her lies.

Instead there was . . . silence.

Caroline cautiously opened her eyes. Phoebe was watching her, a rapt and fascinated look on her face.

"A gaming establishment," she breathed. "Truly, Caro?"

Caroline nodded. "I fear so."

"Oh! It is just like *A Gamble on Love*. You must tell me all about it. What fascinating people you must have met!"

Relief swept over Caroline. She should have known her sister better; Phoebe did not have a condemning bone in her body. But she was far too curious for her own good.

"I certainly will not 'tell you all about it.' The people were generally most unfascinating, too drunk to walk straight, let alone converse. It was a dreadful life, and we are well away from it here."

Phoebe's face, so avid and shining only a moment before, darkened. "Only we will not be here much longer. All because of Lord Lyndon. I suppose he came to your . . . your place frequently, and that is how he knew you. Though I must say it took long enough for him to recognize you."

Caroline shook her head. "I always wore a mask, so no one could recognize me. And it was actually Harry Seward who was a frequent visitor. I only saw Lord Lyndon there twice, once when he came with his brother right after his return from India and then the day after."

"Why did he come then?"

Caroline hesitated. The story of Harry Seward and his fight was so very inappropriate for a young girl's ears. But then, she had already told this particular young girl the rest of the sordid story.

"Mr. Seward had a . . . a disagreement with another patron, which resulted in some furniture breaking."

Phoebe nodded sagely. "A brawl. That sounds like something Harry Seward would do."

"You are not disappointed, dear? I know you are rather fond of him."

"Perhaps I was, once. Now I am through with him and all his family. I suppose Lord Lyndon paid off his brother's debts on that second visit?"

"Yes. When he was there, I tripped." She looked down ruefully at her swollen appendage. "Much like today. He came to my assistance and saw the scar."

"So that is how he knew you," Phoebe murmured. "Oh, my poor, poor Caro! And now we must go away."

Yes. They had to go away. "You can see why, can you not? We will be ruined if we stay."

"Like Mary, I will go with you anywhere you like. You are the best sister in the world, and I have been such a trial to you!" Phoebe threw herself into Caroline's arms, crying contritely, "I will never be any trouble to you again, I swear."

Caroline kissed the top of Phoebe's head and held her close. "You could never be a trial to me, Phoebe. You are all my family now, and I love you."

"I love you, too. And I will help you, I promise. I will make everything better."

"You make things better just by being here."

Phoebe hugged her once more, then stood up and walked toward the door. "I will just go and start my own packing now. I'm supposed to have tea with Sarah later, and I can tell her good-bye then. You just rest, Caro." She smiled and ran off.

Caroline looked after her suspiciously. "Do you believe she is just going to pack, Mary?" she asked.

Mary just pressed the glass of milk and brandy into her hand and said, "Drink this, madam. It will help you feel better."

Chapter Twenty

"I am here to see Lord Lyndon," Phoebe said stoutly, facing down the prune-faced butler with her hands on her hips. "If you please."

The butler's lips flattened even farther, and he kept a firm grip on the door, leaving Phoebe on the doorstep. "His lordship is occupied at the moment, Miss . . ."

"I am Miss Lane."

"Miss Lane. His lordship is occupied at the moment with important business and is not accepting visitors."

Phoebe felt a hot flare of temper in her stomach spreading up until it threatened to burst forth in a torrent of screaming, shouting, and generally unladylike behavior. Her sister was in despair, all because of Lord Lyndon, and he sat smug in his house, guarded by this elderly dragon of a gatekeeper.

She stamped her foot. "*I* happen to have 'important business' with his lordship, and I will see him right now!"

With that, she burst past the shocked butler and through the front door. She dashed down the corridor, looking quickly into the doorways she passed, the butler hard on her heels. For such an old man, he was incredibly quick.

But not quick enough for Phoebe.

She finally found Lord Lyndon in the library, sitting behind a large desk with a decanter of what looked like brandy.

Phoebe marched up to the desk and planted her hands flat on the cool wooden surface. "How dare you, you wicked man!" she shouted.

Justin had been sitting alone in his library with his brandy for about two hours, feeling more and more guilty over his behavior toward Caroline, trying to drown the image of her white, stricken face in the amber liquid's warmth, when he heard the commotion in the foyer. Loud, raised voices, Richards's and a woman's.

Justin shook his head. He hoped it wasn't someone Harry knew, come to cause trouble. He had enough trouble of his own without dealing with Harry's messes.

Then the voices came closer. He heard a rather familiar one insist, "I *will* see Lord Lyndon!"

Miss Lane's voice?

He put the glass carefully back down on the desk. Surely he had not drunk enough of the stuff to be hearing things! His head did not feel in the least bit fuzzy. But not even Miss Lane would come to a gentleman's house and shout at his butler.

Would she?

Then the library door burst open, and Phoebe did indeed stand there. She had changed from her bathing costume into a somewhat respectable bright green gown, but her hair fell down in a mass of curls that positively writhed with indignation.

She strode across the carpet, arms akimbo, then leaned across the desk and shouted, "How dare you, you wicked man!"

Justin just stared up at her frowning face. He had never been called a "wicked man" by a young miss before, and he hardly knew what to say. Should he ask her to sit down? Offer her a brandy? Let her pummel him thoroughly, as she so obviously longed to do?

This was all completely outside his realm of experience. All he could seem to do was stare at her rather stupidly.

Richards appeared at the door, puffing to catch his breath. "My lord," he gasped. "I am so sorry! The young lady . . . she pushed past me. . . ."

Justin rose slowly to his feet. "That is quite all right, Richards. You might fetch my mother, and have some refreshments sent in." Yes. His mother would know what to do.

"Very good, my lord." Richards bowed and gratefully retreated.

Justin turned back reluctantly to face Miss Lane.

She stood with her fists planted on her hips, glaring at him. "This is not a social call. You needn't have ordered refreshments."

Justin propped his hip against the desk and crossed his own arms over his chest. He knew it was quite improper to be in his shirtsleeves, but he didn't want to risk pushing past Medusa to retrieve his coat. "You look as if you have been running a long way. I thought some tea might be in order."

"I don't want anything from you! You are a wi—"

"I know," he interjected dryly. "I am a wicked man."

"You are. A very wicked man. Caroline says we must leave here and go abroad, all because of you. We were happy here, and you ruined everything."

Justin rubbed wearily at his jaw. She was leaving. Leaving. His mind repeated that one word over and over.

"So you knew, too?" he muttered. "Everyone knew the truth but me."

Phoebe shook her head. "I did not know. All these years I thought she was companion to Mr. Aldritch's old aunt. She just told me this afternoon, to explain why we have to leave so quickly."

"And you were not angry that your sister lied to you?"

She looked shocked. "Of course not! Caroline is the very best of sisters. She always has been." Phoebe bit her lip, her eyes suddenly swimming in tears. One drop spilled free, and she wiped it impatiently away. "It was all my fault."

"Your fault?" Justin said sharply. "Why? Were you the one who concocted this scheme to run a gaming establishment, to fleece young men like Harry of their money? To go about in disguise?"

"There is no need to be sarcastic, Lord Lyndon. And Harry is hardly some poor lamb to the slaughter. He practically begs people to take money from his pockets; even I can see that. I am not the stupid little girl everyone thinks me." Phoebe sat down, dropping heavily into the chair beside the desk. "And you are trying to distract me, but it will not work."

This conversation was getting more and more bizarre. Justin wondered if he had fallen asleep at his desk and was having a brandy-induced dream. "Trying to distract you from what, Miss Lane?"

"From my purpose in coming here."

"Which is?"

"To tell you what a looby you are, of course. A wicked looby."

Justin choked. "A—what?"

"A looby." Phoebe shrugged. "It is a word I heard your brother use. And I am sure you are one. You were mean to my sister. She is an absolute angel, and you were cruel to her!"

He *had* been cruel. Justin knew that and was ashamed of it, though, truth to tell, he remembered little of the scene on the shore. He had been in a fog of shock and dismay. "Was I?"

"Caroline would never have done what she did if not for me." Phoebe stared past him, obviously in her own world of recriminations, regrets, and memories. "She hated that Silver Plume place. I could see the revulsion on her face when she spoke of it."

"Golden Feather," Justin automatically corrected.

Phoebe went on as if he had not spoken. "I am sure she would have gone to be a companion to her husband's aunt when he died. But Mrs. Medlock's School, dull as it was, was very expensive. And my clothes, my gewgaws, my pin money." She seized a handful of her green skirt, as if to tear it away. "If I had known, I would not have taken any of those things! I would have left school and taken a position with some other old lady. I would not have let her do that!"

Justin sensed that she was going into hysterics, and looked frantically to the door. Where the deuce *was* his mother?

When Amelia didn't appear, he did the only thing he could think of. He poured a small measure of brandy into a glass and pressed it into her hand.

She sniffled and looked down at it with interest. "Is this brandy?"

"Yes. It will help you calm down."

"I've never had brandy before," she said. Then she gulped it all down.

And promptly began to choke.

"Miss Lane!" Justin thumped her on the back until she stopped wheezing. "You must sip it slowly if you are not accustomed to it."

"You might have told me that before." She eyed the decanter. "May I have some more?"

"Certainly not." Relieved that the coughing, as well as the hysterics, had passed, Justin sat down in a chair across from her. "So Lawrence left your sister no money at all?" he asked, going back to their previous conversation.

Phoebe shook her head. "Not a farthing. Just that . . . that place, which he won in a card game. And, as I said, Mrs. Medlock's was expensive. I would have left there in an instant if Caroline had come for me, but she did not. I am sure she never even considered it. She has always tried to protect me, even when we were children. That is why I have come here today."

Justin was not sure he followed her reasoning. "Why is that, Miss Lane?"

"Because Caroline has always done everything for me. For four years she worked and sacrificed so that I could have a future." Phoebe looked down at where her fist was balled in her skirt. "And today, when I saw how in despair she was, how you hurt her, something inside of me just . . . broke." She smoothed out her skirt and raised her gaze to meet his. "My sister is a lady, Lord Lyndon. The finest lady who ever lived in England, I am sure. I could not allow you, or anyone, to treat her as anything else."

Justin sat back in stunned silence. He had thought Miss Lane to be a rather flighty young woman. But she spoke the truest words he had ever heard, solidifying the vague thoughts that had been floating around in his confused mind all afternoon.

Caroline Aldritch was a true lady. And he had been too blind to see that.

He had thought himself a fool for not seeing that she was Mrs. Archer. Now he knew, like a flash of clarifying light, that he had not really been a fool until the moment he walked away from her on the shore.

The woman he had known these past weeks in Wycombe, the graceful, intelligent, understanding woman he talked to, danced with, and kissed was the real Caroline. And it had been even when she wore the mask of Mrs. Archer.

She was a woman who would live a life she disliked, even hated, for four long years for the love of her sister. If Justin could understand anything, he understood that. Harry was obnoxious at times, yes, but Justin would do anything to keep him safe, to make certain that his future was happy and secure.

Caroline had done the same thing, and he had condemned her for it, abandoned her. Now she was leaving. He had lost her.

Justin groaned and turned his face away from Phoebe, who was crying softly again. In one afternoon, his life had swung in so many different directions he hardly knew where to go.

But he did know that Phoebe was right. He *was* a wicked man, a hypocritical one, who had almost carelessly smashed the lives of the two sisters.

"Caroline says we have to go abroad, because you will tell everyone about the "Copper Quill" and we will be ruined. Not even Sarah will talk to me anymore if I am ruined," Phoebe sobbed. "I don't want to go abroad!"

"You will not have to, Miss Lane. I will never tell anyone."

Phoebe looked up, cautiously hopeful. "Do you promise?"

"I promise, on my father's grave."

She looked as if she wanted to say something else, but his mother came into the room, with Harry close behind her.

"Justin, what is this nonsense Richards says about Miss Lane being in here with—" Amelia broke off when she saw the young lady actually sitting there. "Oh. Good afternoon, Miss Lane."

Phoebe gave a long sniffle. "G-good afternoon, Lady Lyndon."

Harry looked about, bewildered, at Phoebe's tearstained face, the brandy on the desk, and Justin in his shirtsleeves. His youthful face hardened. "You utter cad!" he shouted. "Taking advantage of an innocent lady!"

Before Justin could even guess what he was about, Harry leaped forward, grabbed him by the cravat, and dragged him to the floor.

Justin tried to seize his brother and push him off,

but Harry had the strength of his anger behind him, and clung with terrierlike tenacity. His fist flew out and caught Justin on the cheekbone.

"Dash it, Harry!" Justin shouted. "Get off me, you fool, and I will explain."

"Explain what, you despoiler of virgins!"

"Stop it, boys!" Amelia cried, running around them in a flurry of pale gray skirts. "Stop it this moment!"

Phoebe threw herself into the fray, pummeling Harry with her small fists. "Mr. Seward, no! He was *not* despoiling me. I came here myself." She pulled at his hair.

Harry looked up at her. "Do you mean to say that . . . that you *like* him? My brother?"

"Of course not. He is much too old for me! I came here to talk to him about my sister."

"Oh." Harry released his grip on Justin and stood up. "I am sorry, Justin."

Justin also stood, and tried to rearrange his rumpled attire. His cheek ached like the very devil, and he was sure a nice bruise was forming there. "I suppose you were only defending the lady. But do not let it happen again."

Amelia picked up the brandy from the desk and poured herself out a generous measure. "I must say I am heartily ashamed of you both. Fighting in our own home!" She tossed back the drink with a deep sigh, her shoulders visibly relaxing. "Now see what you have driven me to? Drinking spirits in the middle of the day! I was going to ask you to come to the tea shop with me for strawberries and cake, but now I think Miss Lane and I will go by ourselves. Shall we, Miss Lane?"

Phoebe jumped up eagerly, her earlier tears obviously forgotten in all the excitement. "Oh, yes, please, Lady Lyndon!"

But as Amelia ushered Phoebe out the door, she turned back to level one last stern glance at her sons. "This is not over, Harry, Justin. I will want a thorough explanation of this scene when I get back."

"Yes, Mother," they murmured in a chagrined chorus.

Chapter Twenty-One

The shore was deserted at that time of day; all the bathers and strollers had gone home for their tea. Justin relished the quiet as he stood there on the sand, waves reaching for him but not quite catching him. There, in the silence and the sweet sea air, he felt like the fog that had shrouded his brain was finally lifted, and he could see his way clear.

He loved Caroline. He loved her as Mrs. Aldritch, or Mrs. Archer. Hell, she could call herself Mrs. Tiddlywinks if she liked and he would *still* love her.

He could slap himself for being such an idiot after hearing Phoebe's story, which only confirmed what he had known, deep inside, to be true all along. If Larry, who Justin well knew had not been the most reliable of men, had only left his wife a gaming establishment and a handful of debts, what choice did she have? Would he rather she starved to death in some genteel garret and her sister with her?

"Never," he whispered to himself.

Instead of starving, she had shown herself to be a resourceful and shrewd businesswoman. She had run the Golden Feather with a flair and a panache that no man could ever have matched; she had made it the most successful gaming house in all London.

And she had not done it out of some perverse desire to be shocking, as Justin's first, irrational reaction had been on hearing the truth. No woman with Caroline's innate seriousness and dignity would do that, and he had been an idiot to think so for even an instant.

She had done everything she did out of love, so that her sister could have a happy, respectable life.

He turned his back to the sea to look at her house in the distance. He was on his way there, to apologize, to grovel on his very knees if necessary. But now that the moment was upon him he was a coward. He had no idea what to say, what words might bring her back to him. He was afraid he would forget everything he wanted to say, and just fall on the floor and sob at her feet.

Getting her shoes all wet would hardly endear him to her.

He sensed that this was the most important, the most vital conversation he would ever have in his life. And he had to have it now, before she left Wycombe, her sister and her luggage in tow, and he never saw her again.

Justin smoothed down his windblown hair, tugged his cravat into place, and walked toward her house.

A knock sounded at the door.

Caroline, tucking a stack of chemises into a trunk, looked up impatiently and blew a stray lock of hair out of her eyes.

"Oh, who could that be?" she muttered. "I don't have time for callers, with all these clothes still to be packed."

She listened for Mary or the new housemaid to answer the door, but there was no sound. They must still be in the kitchen, arguing with the cook over supper.

Then there was another knock.

Caroline pushed the rest of the garments into the trunk, reached for her makeshift walking stick, and stood up to go answer the blighted thing herself. The sooner she sent whoever it was away, the sooner she could finish her packing.

And the sooner they could leave Wycombe.

She was halfway down the stairs when Mary came hurrying across the small, trunk-filled foyer, murmuring and shaking her head.

The maid opened the door, and shouted, "You! We don't want to see the likes of *you* here! Go away."

She started to slam the door, but a booted foot was thrust between the stout wood and the frame, preventing it from closing.

"Please, Mary," a deep voice said. "I know I am not your favorite person at the moment, but I must see Mrs. Aldritch."

"You *must* go away!" Mary pushed her slight figure against the door, but he was well wedged.

Justin. Justin had come to see her.

Caroline pressed her hand against the sudden fluttering at the base of her throat. What could he want? To shout at her, threaten her? To warn her to stay away from his family before she tainted them with the stench of the Golden Feather?

She knew she should send him away, that she

should not subject herself to any more of the pain his condemnation brought. But her curiosity—and the wild desire to see him just once more—won out over self-preservation.

"Mary," she called, coming the rest of the way down the stairs, "it is quite all right. You can let Lord Lyndon in."

Mary looked up, her cap askew over one eye. "But, madam . . ."

"I will deal with him," Caroline said.

"Please, Caroline!" Justin called. "I only want to talk to you."

Mary stepped suddenly away from the door, causing Justin, whose entire weight was against the wood, to tumble ignominiously onto the foyer floor. He sprawled most inelegantly on the black-and-white tile.

Mary looked down at him and sniffed. "Talk, then, your lordship," she said scornfully. "But don't expect any tea."

Then she stalked off, back to the kitchen.

Caroline bit her lip uncertainly as she watched Justin scramble to his feet, his elegant attire all in disarray. She didn't know if she should laugh at the sight, or cry. So she just said, "Shall we go into the drawing room?"

Justin nodded, as dignified as he could be with his hair all tumbled about. "Thank you."

Caroline drew her shawl about her shoulders and limped her way into the drawing room, closing the door behind them against any prying ears. As he moved past her, she smelled the warm sun caught on the wool of his coat, a spicy scent, and a tang that was only Justin. And . . . something else.

Brandy? Was he foxed, and that was what made him come to her?

"Have you been drinking?" she blurted before she could catch herself.

He turned to look at her, a rueful half smile on his lips. "Just a bit. Have you?"

Caroline felt an equally rueful expression steal across her own face. "A bit. Mary put brandy in the milk."

"Good. Then we will be equally incoherent."

Caroline sat down on the settee beside the window, holding herself stiff and still. "Why have you come here? I thought we said everything there was to say this afternoon."

Justin shifted on one foot, looking every bit as uncomfortable as she herself felt. "I had a visitor this afternoon."

"Who was it?"

"Miss Lane."

"Phoebe?" Caroline cried. Phoebe had gone alone to Justin's house? She knew her sister was rather, well, *impulsive,* but this was the outside of enough. "She told me she was going to tea with Miss Bellweather."

"I daresay she *is* at tea now. My mother took her to the tea shop for cake and strawberries. But on the way she made a small stop in my library."

Caroline looked down at her lap, twisting and smoothing the pale blue muslin of her skirt. Now he would think her a terribly irresponsible chaperon on top of everything else. "I do apologize."

"There is no need for that. She taught me a very valuable lesson."

She gaped up at him in surprise. "A lesson? Phoebe? What could that have been?"

"That I am a wicked looby, of course," he said in a strangely blithe tone.

"A—what?"

"A wicked looby. Those were her words."

"Oh, Justin—Lord Lyndon—she should not have done that." Caroline could have sunk to the floor in profound embarrassment.

"Of course she should have. I heartily deserved it for . . . well, for my loobyish behavior. If there is such a word." He came over to her and knelt beside her settee. His hair brushed silkily against her fingers, his fragrance and warmth wrapped around her. "She also taught me the value of true loyalty. And that brings me to what I came here to say."

Caroline linked her fingers tightly together to keep from twining them in his hair. "What did you come here to say?"

"That I am sorry. So very sorry, Caroline."

Were her ears deceiving her? Or maybe she was dreaming. Surely he, the Earl of Lyndon, could not be kneeling here on her floor, telling her he was sorry.

"You . . . are sorry?" she managed to whisper.

His eyes were ablaze with the blue heat of a summer's sky as he looked up at her. "I was so . . . so shocked when I saw the truth. My damnable Seward pride was hurt. I was convinced that you had set out to deceive me, to make a fool of me."

"I did not!" Caroline cried. "I wanted so many times to tell you the truth these last weeks. But I didn't. I couldn't."

"You had your sister to protect."

"Yes. If I had told you, we would have been ruined. I don't mind that so much for myself; I would like a quiet country life, away from society. But Phoebe is innocent, and she deserves to decide her own fate." She shook her head. "Even that would not have held me back much longer, I'm afraid. Once I realized how . . . how very serious things were becoming between us, I determined to tell you the truth. I tried to this morning, before I fell."

"You did. But then I saw that scar, and I reacted like a complete idiot. I did not see the obvious."

"I never set out to use you or your family," Caroline said. "I just liked your mother so much, and even Harry, too, began to grow on me."

"And me?" he said, his voice boyishly hopeful. "Did you like me?"

"Oh, yes," she answered softly. Then she gave in to her yearning to touch him, placing her hands softly on either side of his face, framing his beloved features. The prickle of his afternoon whiskers tickled at her palms. "How could I help but like you? You were everything I ever dreamed about but thought could not possibly exist."

"Do you like me still?" he whispered.

"Justin," she whispered back, "I love you."

He raised up on his knees and kissed her, his mouth moving softly, sweetly against hers. Then she wrapped her arms around him, and he pressed closer, his lips parting to meet hers.

Eventually he drew back, his eyes heavy with desire as he looked at her. Both of them were gasping for breath, and Caroline slid off the settee to sit on the floor beside him. He rested his head in her lap, clutching at her skirts as if he feared she might escape him.

"Oh, Caroline," he murmured. "Why could I not have met you years ago?"

Caroline stroked the hair back from his brow and laughed softly. "You would have had to come to Devonshire. Were you ever in Devonshire?"

"Not that I know of."

"Well, that is where I was."

"But if I had met you then, I would never have gone to India. You never would have married Larry. We could have sixteen children by now."

"I do not think it works that way. We were not the same people then that we are now. I was very young and silly when I married Lawrence. I did not make a good wife."

"Will you tell me about it?"

Caroline let her head fall back against the edge of the settee, reluctantly remembering. "My family was a good one, an old one, but they had little in the way of . . . of material comfort. We lived quite shabbily in the country, and I knew that my parents expected that I would improve their fortunes with a good marriage. They were trying to scrape together enough money for my Season."

"But you wed Larry instead."

"His family, whose estate was very near ours, was much in the same situation as ours. They had a good name, but little money. Lawrence's father had problems with gaming, and I think his mother did, too. They wanted, needed, an heiress for their son. But we were in love. Or thought we were. We often met in secret. It felt very thrilling."

"And what happened?"

"We eloped, of course. Made a dash for Gretna Green. When we came back, our parents were furi-

ous. All their plans were ruined, and not even my
mother, who really was fond of me in her own
way, could help. They disowned us, so we went to
London. Lawrence had some vague idea of getting
work of some sort."

"How long was it before you realized Larry had
the same . . . the same problem as his parents?"

"Gaming, you mean? Not very long. He would
often go out at night, leaving me alone in our
shabby little lodgings. I suppose he was with you
and his other friends."

Justin winced against her skirt. "He said his wife
did not mind that he was out so late."

"I *did* mind, but I did not say anything. I was
still silly and in love."

"When did things change?"

"We had been married a little over a year. I
was *enceinte*, and Lawrence was drinking heavily.
Losing money heavily, too. I had to hide coins from
him so I could buy food and coal. Then, one night,
he found out what I was doing. We quarreled,
shouted. Lawrence was never physically violent
with me, but that night he had been drinking. He
broke a vase, and I fell. I cut my ankle open on
the shards, and I-I lost the baby."

She closed her eyes tightly. It still hurt, the memory of that long-ago night.

Justin reached out and touched her ankle, laying
his palm flat against the raised scar beneath the
silk stocking.

"I am so sorry," he said simply.

"It was for the best, really. That was no life for
a child. And certainly the Golden Feather would
not have been!"

"Did you hate the place so very much?"

Caroline thought about this question carefully, her mind winding around the past. "I hated men trying to grab my backside as I walked past them, and drunken people getting loud and angry when they lost. But I did not hate the place itself. It meant independence and the possibility of a future for Phoebe and myself. It was Lawrence's last, best gift to me. No, I did not hate it."

As she suddenly realized that truth, she felt freer and lighter than she had in years. She could acknowledge the past, and let it go. Lawrence, the lost baby, the Golden Feather—it all flew away.

She looked down at Justin, lying in her lap.

"The Golden Feather brought me you," she said lightly. "How can I hate it?"

He turned his face up to her and kissed her quickly on the chin. "I think you are the bravest person I have ever met."

Caroline felt herself turning pink. "Brave? Certainly not. I only did what I had to in order to survive. *You* were brave to go to India and face tigers and snakes. I never could have done that, not even for Phoebe."

He laughed ruefully. "I went to India because my father sent me there after I fought three duels."

"You fought three duels? Never! I can't believe it."

"Oh, believe it. I was quite the young hellion. I put Harry to shame. My father didn't know what else to do with me, so off I went." He fell silent for a moment, stroking a bit of her soft muslin skirt between his fingers. "I hated India at first, and I hated my father for sending me there. But now I am deeply grateful to him. It made me stronger, more independent. It made me see what is truly important in life."

"And what is that?"

"Family. And true honor. And love." He reached up and drew her head down to his for another long, lingering kiss. "Especially love."

"Umm, yes," Caroline murmured with a smile. "I do see what you mean."

"So I suppose it was a good thing we did not meet years ago."

"No. We would have been too careless to see what we had."

"And now that we are older, our marriage will be stronger."

Caroline, who had been leaning down for another kiss, froze. "Marriage?"

Justin laughed. "Of course marriage! You did not think I was offering you *carte blanche,* did you? After all the groveling and apologizing I have done?"

"No. I did not think that." Caroline carefully moved him aside and got up to sit back down on the settee. "But I did not think of *marriage,* either. Not seriously, anyway. To be your countess . . ."

Justin sat up, a fierce, puzzled frown on his face. "Then what exactly were you thinking?"

That was a very good question, and it was not one that Caroline had an answer for. Truly, she had not been thinking at all. She loved Justin, longed for him, but she had thought that with her secret they could never wed. Now all was revealed, and he wanted to marry her anyway.

She looked at him and saw that he offered everything she had ever wanted. Love, family, a title, a home, respectability. He held it out to her on the palm of his hand, and all she had to do was reach out and pick it up.

She wanted, more than she had ever wanted anything, to be selfish, to reach out and take it, and damn the consequences.

But she loved him too much. Too much to marry him, to risk someone else finding out the truth, and spreading it far and wide that the Countess of Lyndon was once the owner of a gaming hell. The Sewards were an old and proud family. She would not destroy them, or the man she loved.

A sharp pain clawed at her belly as she thought of the life, the children they could have had. But looking after others before herself was too deeply ingrained.

She closed her eyes and shook her head. "I cannot marry you."

"What!" He leaped to his feet. "Then what is this all about? I love you, Caroline. I thought you loved me."

"I *do* love you!" she cried. "That is why I cannot marry you."

"I do not understand."

"What if someone discovered the truth? The scandal would be a hundred times worse if I were the Countess of Lyndon than if I were just plain Mrs. Aldritch. Don't you see?"

A pulse ticked in Justin's jaw. He was obviously furious, more furious than Caroline had ever seen him. "No, I do not see."

"I will not be the cause of scandal for your family. I care about all of you too much."

"You are being ridiculous," Justin said tightly. "No one knows of this but you, me, and your maid and sister. I hardly think *they* will go gossiping about it."

"*You* found out! Someone else could as well."

"I only found out because I saw your scar. Did you go about flashing it at everyone?"

"Of course not!"

"Of course not. And not even Harry, who met you on several occasions as Mrs. Archer, has recognized you."

"I cannot take that chance."

Justin looked as if he would very much like to say something else. His mouth opened and closed again.

Finally, he said, "All right, then, Caroline. Be all self-sacrificing if you want to. But this is not the end. I will come back, again and again, until you agree to marry me."

Then he turned on his heel and left. The front door closed with a loud snap behind him, and Caroline was all alone in the echoing silence.

"I am *not* self-sacrificing," she muttered, hitting at a cushion with her fist. "I am *sensible*."

Chapter Twenty-Two

"It was awful!" Phoebe whispered to Sarah and
Harry. The three of them were huddled together
on the last row of chairs at Mrs. Stone's musicale,
whispering and murmuring beneath the loud
screech of Miss Stone's violin solo. "I was just
going up the walkway to our front door when Lord
Lyndon came bursting out. His face was all red,
and he was muttering to himself. He walked right
past me without saying a word. I would vow he did
not even see me."

Harry squirmed uncomfortably in his seat, but
Sarah's brown eyes were wide with interest. "What
did you find when you went inside?" she asked.

"My sister was in the drawing room, just sitting
there all quiet. But I could see she had been crying." Phoebe sighed. "I thought I was helping by
going to speak to Lord Lyndon. It seems I have
only made things worse. Something tragic has happened to separate them!" She shot a sharp glance
at Harry. "If only *someone* had not lost his temper
and started a fight. I know I was getting through
to Lord Lyndon, given just a bit more time."

"Me!" cried Harry. Several people looked over

at them, and he quickly lowered his voice. "Me? I was only coming to your rescue."

"I did not need to be rescued. I was just starting to make some progress." Phoebe turned her gaze to where Caroline sat, ostensibly listening to the music. She never moved her eyes from Miss Stone and her violin. Then Phoebe looked at Lord Lyndon, sitting with his mother and Lady Bellweather on the opposite side of the room from Caroline. He, too, pretended great interest in the terrible music, but he kept darting little looks at Caroline.

"Now it is all ruined," Phoebe continued. "Caro gave up the scheme of leaving Wycombe the very next day, but she says we will go at the end of the week." Phoebe did not want to leave, or at least she did not want to go back to Devonshire as Caroline was talking of doing. She wanted to go to Brighton with Sarah, or maybe to London.

And she wanted her sister to be happy. It hurt her heart every time she saw Caroline drifting about the house, pale and sad. She wasn't certain what had happened between Caroline and Lord Lyndon three days ago, but she was sure there must be something she could do to make things right. The two of them so obviously cared for each other. It was ridiculous and tragic for them to be apart, just like in *Lady Lucinda's Passion*.

"Did your brother say anything to you about what happened?" she asked Harry.

"Not a word," he answered. "But Justin has been an absolute bear ever since. I spilled some tea at breakfast, and you would have thought I burned down the house from the way he shouted!" Harry sighed. "I vow I will be glad to rusticate at Seward Park after this."

Phoebe tapped her finger thoughtfully on her chin. "There must be *something* we can do to help, since they are too bacon brained to do it themselves. Come, help me devise a scheme."

The three of them bent their heads together.

Harry and Phoebe and Sarah were up to something, Justin could tell.

In between stealing glances at Caroline, he watched them. They had been whispering, thick as thieves, at the back of the room ever since the music (if one could call it that) began. After the smugglers' treasure contretemps and all the little mischiefs since, Justin did not trust them one whit.

But he did wish he still had some of their aptitude for scheming. If he did, he could come up with a plan to get Caroline to marry him.

Not that he had even tried. In the three days since the scene in her drawing room, he had lain awake every night, devising wild and unlikely plans to win her. In the clear light of day, they all looked extremely ridiculous. Caroline's mind was made up; she was obviously doing what she felt was right, and all the letters and bouquets he sent would not move her.

If only he could make her see that nothing mattered, nothing but her! No one would ever find out about Mrs. Archer, and even if they did it would not matter. He would just take her and all their family to stay at Waring Castle, and the scandal would die the natural death of a nine days' wonder.

What he needed was a really good plan, something romantic, something that would prove to her his sincerity. . . .

His gaze snapped back to the whispering young trio.

As the violin piece ended and relieved applause broke out, Justin rose from his chair and went to the back row where the three of them were sitting.

Their alarmed glances and sudden silence proved to him that he had indeed been the subject of their conversation.

"Harry, ladies," he said, sitting down beside them, "I wonder if I might beg your assistance. . . ."

Oh, Lord, would this evening never end?

Caroline sat very still, her hands folded in her lap, her eyes aimed forward to the young lady and her violin, a polite mask on her face. But she was all too aware of Justin watching her, trying to catch her attention, and her mind was racing wildly from one thought to another.

She longed to go home, to shut herself away in her room, alone. Maybe there, in the quiet, she could sort out her thoughts.

Then again, maybe not.

She had been trying to sort them for three days, three days of steadfastly avoiding Justin, and they had insisted on remaining in chaos.

She told herself over and over that she was doing the right thing. If she gave in to her selfish desires and agreed to marry Justin, they would be happy for a while. But eventually he would come to resent her past, especially if it caused a scandal. He would become cold, would turn to other women, maybe to drink as Lawrence had. She had seen such things over and over among the *ton*nish patrons of the Golden Feather. Men who gambled until the wee hours to avoid going home, masked women with wedding bands on their fingers who drank and laughed with forced gaiety.

A life of that sort would kill her. It would be more painful to have a life with Justin and lose it than any pain she was going through now could be.

At least that was what she told herself. Repeatedly.

If only he would cease sending her flowers and notes, reminding her of his presence! If only he would accept that what she was doing was for his benefit, and go away to his castle.

A burst of applause broke out around her, and she realized with a start that the music was over. She looked about, and saw that Justin was gone from his seat.

Caroline rose to her feet, relieved, and was about to go seek some refreshments when she saw her sister and Sarah Bellweather coming toward her. Phoebe had one gloved hand pressed dramatically to her brow.

"Oh, Caro!" she cried. "May we please go home now? I have such a dreadful headache."

"A headache?" Caroline said in alarm. Phoebe was never ill; she was always far too busy for fits of the megrims. She took off one glove and laid her fingers against Phoebe's forehead. "You *are* rather warm, and your cheeks are flushed."

"It came upon her very suddenly," Sarah offered. "She could hardly rise from her seat."

"Miss Stone's violin and this heat are enough to give anyone a headache," Caroline said. She even felt one throbbing at the back of her own head now. "Let us just say good-bye to our hostess; then we can be off. Mary will know of a posset for you."

"And can Sarah come, too?" Phoebe said, leaning weakly against Caroline's arm.

"It is quite all right with my mother," Sarah said. "We already asked her."

Caroline peered at Phoebe closely. "You felt well enough to walk across the room and speak to Lady Bellweather before coming back here to me?"

Phoebe gave a pitiable little smile. "It would make me feel *ever* so much better to have Sarah with me."

Caroline was too tired to argue. "Oh, very well, then. Come along, girls."

Phoebe's chamber, unlike Caroline's, had a window that faced the street. When Caroline and Sarah went to tuck her up in her bed, she insisted that the curtains be left open.

"But you will be disturbed by the noise from the street," Caroline protested. "That is not good for a headache."

"I-I like the light," Phoebe said, leaning back against her pillows.

"All right, then." Caroline, who had been in the process of closing the satin curtains, reopened them, and went to give her sister a kiss. "I will leave you and Sarah to retire, then."

Phoebe's gaze darted past her, toward the small clock hung above her fireplace mantel. "Oh, no!"

Caroline drew back to look at her. "What do you mean no? Phoebe, you are acting very oddly." She was surely up to something, Caroline could tell. Her cheeks were red with a hectic flush, and Sarah

Bellweather's brown eyes were far too wide and innocent.

They were most assuredly up to some mischief.

"I, well, I just mean don't go yet," Phoebe said with a little laugh. "I would like some . . . some warm milk. To help me sleep."

"I will ring for Mary, then," Caroline said, reaching for the embroidered bellpull.

"But you make it ever so much better!" Phoebe said beseechingly. "You make it much better than Mary does."

Caroline regarded Phoebe with narrowed eyes. Now she *knew* something was afoot. The minx could not be planning to elope with Harry Seward, could she? Perhaps she meant to climb down from her window and jump into a carriage with him as soon as Caroline's back was turned. To make a run for Gretna Green, as she had done herself so long ago.

Well, they would just see about that.

"Very well," she said. "I will go fetch the milk. But you had best be here when I return."

"Why, Caro!" Phoebe cried, all innocence. "Where would I go?"

Caroline gave her one last warning glance, then hurried downstairs, sending Mary back up to keep a sharp eye on the girls while she made the milk. It took longer than expected to heat the milk and find cinnamon and cloves to grate into it while avoiding the cook's irate questions about why she was in the kitchen, so it was fully fifteen minutes before she returned to Phoebe's chamber.

There she found the window overlooking the street wide open, and Phoebe, Mary, and Sarah all leaning over the sill looking down.

And floating up to them was a sound egregious enough to rival even Miss Stone's violin playing.

The strains of some stringed instrument, a lute or a mandolin perhaps, were discernible, and above them rose a voice of unimaginable unmusicality.

" 'When Nature made her chief work, Stella's eyes, In color black, why wrapp'd she beams so bright?' " the voice warbled. " 'Would she in beamy black, like painter wise, Frame daintiest lustre, mixed of shades and light?' "

Caroline put the glass down on a table and went over to the window, hardly aware of her own feet moving, carrying her forward.

Surely this could not be what she thought.

The three women parted at her approach, hovering at either side of the window with silly, giggling grins on their faces. Caroline leaned over the sill and looked down.

Justin stood on the pavement outside the house, singing as loudly as he possibly could and gesturing broadly with his arms. Behind him stood Harry, strumming inexpertly but enthusiastically on a lute.

They had gathered quite a crowd of interested onlookers about them, as well, some of them people Caroline recognized from the musicale. Perhaps they thought this was merely a continuation of the party.

Against her will, Caroline felt a silly grin spreading slowly across her own face. Then a laugh rose up in her throat, and another and another. She could not help it; he looked so very comical, and so dear.

And so scandalous. Everyone in Wycombe would know of this scene by morning, and it would be greatly exaggerated as well. Earls simply did not sing beneath respectable women's windows, causing scenes. It just wasn't done.

Perhaps he was foxed, and Harry, too. But Caroline only remembered a weak claret cup being served at the musicale, and they had not been gone long enough to go to some tavern.

" 'Both so and thus, she, minding Love should be Placed ever there, gave him this mourning weed, To honor all their deaths, who for her bleed.' "

His song at an end, Justin fell silent.

"Whatever are you doing, Lord Lyndon?" Caroline called, trying to sound stern despite her helpless laughter.

In answer, Justin fell to his knees, one hand clasped over his heart. Harry laid down his lute and reached into a basket at his feet for a handful of flowers, which he tossed up to her window. Some fell back to the ground and some hit her in the face.

She clutched at the blossoms, her gaze never leaving Justin's face.

"Can't you see, Caroline?" he called back. "I am willing to cause any scene, any scandal, for you. If you refuse my proposal again tonight, I will just come back tomorrow, and the night after that, and the night after that, until you hear me out. I do not care about anything but you, and I never will."

The collective gaze of the gathered crowd swung from him up to her window. Phoebe, Mary, and Sarah were all happily crying against each other's shoulders.

"It is just so romantic," Mary sobbed.

"Like *The Romance of the Ruby Chalice*," Phoebe sniffled.

Caroline saw and heard none of this. The stares, the whispers—it was everything she feared, everything she had hoped she left behind at the Golden Feather. But somehow she didn't care about any of it.

She only cared about Justin and what he was doing for her. Earls were meant to be dignified and elegant, and he acted the abject clown right in the middle of the street. All for her, to gain her attention.

She had been a fool, she saw that so clearly now, to ever hold propriety above love. A silly fool, so blinded by her past that she could not see the truth that was right there before her.

Justin had faced down scandal in his own past, and he was not afraid of it. He was too strong for that, and she had underestimated him.

She would never do that again.

Tears were falling warmly, silently down her cheeks. She buried her face in the fragrance of the flowers she held.

"Well, Caroline?" she heard Justin say. "Shall I sing again? I only know the one song."

Caroline looked up and laughed. "Certainly not! We do not want poor Sir Phillip Sidney to rise from his grave in protest."

"I will only not sing again if you will let me come in and talk to you."

Caroline looked at his beloved face, bathed in moonlight and hope. Yes, she *had* been a fool to think she could ever leave him.

She was a fool no longer. "I will do more than that," she answered. "I will marry you."

All the onlookers burst into applause, while Phoebe and Sarah danced a little happy dance, waltzing each other around the room.

Justin rose slowly from his knees. "Say that again," he said in a strangled voice.

"I will marry you!" she shouted happily.

Justin ran up the front steps then and through the door that Mary had gone down to obligingly hold open for him.

Caroline spun about and dashed out of the room. They met halfway up the staircase, and Justin caught her against him in a kiss that no woman could be foolish enough to leave again. He lifted her off her feet, and she wound her arms about his neck, clinging as if she would never let go.

Justin pulled back and leaned his forehead against hers. "I just want to be certain I heard you correctly. Did you say you would marry me?"

"I did, and I will."

"When?"

"Tomorrow?"

"A dash for Gretna Green?"

Caroline hesitated, but then nodded. "If you like."

"Of course I would like it! To have you as my wife within days would be heaven. But I could not do that to you. Your first wedding was an elopement. This time you should have all the gewgaws."

"Like cake!" a voice cried. "And champagne."

"And rose petals!"

They looked up to see Phoebe and Sarah hanging over the banister, watching them with avid young eyes.

"And we want to be bridesmaids," Phoebe added. "In orange silk."

"No, blue," said Sarah.

"All right, then. Blue." Phoebe sighed happily.

"It will be just like *Lady Arabella's Royal Wedding*."

"You see, now, Caroline dear," Justin said. "We must have a grand wedding. We could never disappoint two such lovely, and helpful, young ladies. Could we?"

"I suppose not. A grand wedding it is, then."

"In the autumn? At Waring Castle?"

Caroline nodded and actually giggled in her soaring delight. "Autumn. And not a day later!"

Then she leaned her head against his shoulder and closed her eyes. Safe. She was safe at last. After all the years of searching, of loneliness, she would never be alone or fearful again.

Epilogue

October, Waring Castle

"It is all so lovely," Phoebe said, her voice rhapsodic. "Just like . . ."

"The Sins of Madame Evelyn?" suggested Harry.

"I would wager it is *The Enchanted Vale,*" said Sarah.

"You are both wrong," protested Phoebe. "I was going to say it is just like a . . . a fairy tale. Like the ones Caro read to me when I was very little."

Indeed it was. The three of them stood at the edge of the grand ballroom at Waring Castle, watching the dancers swirl and twirl in the figures of a waltz. Bright silks and satins and flashing jewels created a kaleidoscope of color and motion. Music soared to the sky blue–painted dome above, and the scent of flowers hung sweetly in the cool autumn air.

It *was* like a scene from a fairy tale, a royal ball on the eve of a glorious wedding.

And at the center of it all were a prince and princess, or rather an earl and a countess-to-be.

Phoebe watched her sister dancing in the arms of her almost-husband, looking radiant and happy in a gown of emerald green silk, and she gave a smug smile. Without her help, things would not have reached this most satisfactory conclusion, and she was feeling quite smart indeed.

Surely there were other people who could benefit from her help. She would just have to look about for them, after her wedding duties were concluded.

"I suppose we will not see each other again until Christmas, Phoebe," Harry said to her quietly.

She turned and smiled at him. Dear Harry. How very dashing he looked tonight, in his red-and-gold striped waistcoat and red coat. It went so well with her own coral-colored ensemble. "I suppose we will not," she answered lightly. "You are off to take charge of Seward Park, and I will be staying with Sarah and her family while my sister is on her wedding trip to Scotland."

Harry shifted on his feet, uncharacteristically shy. "But . . . well. Dash it, that is, will you write to me, Phoebe? While I am gone?"

Phoebe laughed and tucked her hand in the crook of his elbow. "Of course I will write to you, Harry! We are family now."

"Are you happy tonight, Caroline dearest?" Justin swung his bride-to-be in a wide circle, making her skirts shimmer in an emerald fire.

She tightened her grip on his shoulder and laughed merrily. For the first time in many, many years she felt free. Free and light and young. In his arms, she knew she could soar. "Happier than I have ever been."

"And this is only the beginning."

"Oh, yes! Only the beginning."

Signet Regency Romances from

BARBARA METZGER

"Barbara Metzger deliciously mixes love and laughter." —*Romantic Times*

MISS WESTLAKE'S WINDFALL
0-451-20279-1

Miss Ada Westlake has two treasures at her fingertips. One is a cache of coins she discovered in her orchard, and the other is her friend (and sometime suitor), Viscount Ashmead. She has been advised to keep a tight hold on both. But Ada must discover for herself that the greatest gift of all is true love....

THE PAINTED LADY
0-451-20368-2

Stunned when the lovely lady he is painting suddenly comes to life on the canvas and talks to him, the Duke of Caswell can only conclude that his mind has finally snapped. But when his search for help sends him to Sir Osgood Bannister, the noted brain fever expert and doctor to the king, he ends up in the care of the charming, naive Miss Lilyanne Bannister, and his life suddenly takes on a whole new dimension...

To order call: 1-800-788-6262

Signet Regency Romances from

ELISABETH FAIRCHILD

"An outstanding talent."
—*Romantic Times*

CAPTAIN CUPID CALLS THE SHOTS
0-451-20198-1

Captain Alexander Shelbourne was known as Cupid to his friends for his uncanny marksmanship in battle. But upon meeting Miss Penny Foster, he soon knew how it felt to be struck by his namesake's arrow....

SUGARPLUM SURPRISES
0-451-20421-2

Lovely Jane Nichol—who spends her days disguised as a middle-aged seamstress—has crossed paths with a duke who shelters a secret as great as her own. But as Christmas approaches—and vicious rumors surface—they begin to wonder if they can have their cake and eat it, too...

To order call: 1-800-788-6262

Allison Lane

"A FORMIDABLE TALENT...
MS. LANE NEVER FAILS TO
DELIVER THE GOODS."
—*ROMANTIC TIMES*

THE NOTORIOUS WIDOW
0-451-20166-3
When a scoundrel tries to tarnish a young widow's reputation, a valiant Earl tries to repair the damage—and mend her broken heart as well...

BIRDS OF A FEATHER
0-451-19825-5
When a plain, bespectacled young woman keeps meeting the handsome Lord Wylie, she feels she is not up to his caliber. A great arbiter of fashion for London society, Lord Wylie was reputed to be more interseted in the cut of his clothes than the feelings of others, as the young woman bore witness to. Degraded by him in public, she could nevertheless forget his dashing demeanor. It will take a public scandal, and a private passion, to bring them together...

To order call: 1-800-788-6262